#3

star power

Never Give Up

Catch Star's act!

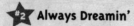
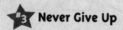
A new book drops every other month!
Next up:

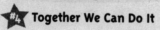
From Aladdin Paperbacks
Published by Simon & Schuster

star power

Never Give Up

by Catherine Hapka

Aladdin Paperbacks

New York London Toronto Sydney

First Aladdin Paperbacks edition July 2004

Copyright © 2004 by Catherine Hapka

ALADDIN PAPERBACKS
An imprint of Simon & Schuster
Children's Publishing Division
1230 Avenue of the Americas
New York, NY 10020

Designed by Debra Sfetsios
The text of this book was set in Berkeley Book.

Printed in the United States of America
2 4 6 8 10 9 7 5 3 1

Library of Congress Control Number 2003096182

ISBN 0-689-86789-1

star power

Never Give Up

One

From: singingstar0I

To: MissTaka

Subject: Guess where I am right now?!?!

Hi Missy,

U'll never guess where I am as I'm writing this. I mean, u prob'ly know I'm in Milan b/c I told u that in my e-mail yesterday. But guess where I am RIGHT NOW?

OK, give up? Then I'll tell u—I'm at a fashion show! The designer is that Italian guy, Ceasario Pucci—u know, the I who invented the scratch-and-smell purse. He sent an invite after my concert here in Milan last night. Now I'm sitting in the front row checking out oodles of awesome new fashions! 2 cool 4 words!!!!

Better sign off now—don't want anyone 2 think I'm not paying attention. I'll write u later w/all the details.

Luv ya,

Star

Star Calloway hit a button on her handheld computer to send the e-mail she'd just typed to her best friend. Then she glanced up quickly, not wanting to miss a moment of the fashion show. She was sitting in a folding chair just a couple of feet from the edge of a raised catwalk. Strobe lights bounced around the crowded room, and loud, pulsing music throbbed from large speakers suspended over the stage. Every few seconds a different model stepped out from behind a purple velvet curtain and pranced down the catwalk showing off yet another outrageous high-fashion outfit.

Star leaned over to check on her dog, Dudley Do-Wrong. The little fawn pug was under her chair taking a nap, completely oblivious to the noise and commotion going on around him. Luckily his snores were drowned out by the loud music.

Suddenly the crowd murmured with excitement. Star sat up and looked at the model who had just stepped out onto the catwalk. The newcomer was very tall and very thin, with lustrous waves of dark hair, flawless olive skin, and startlingly green eyes. She was wearing an outrageous dress composed mostly of plastic spiders, with weblike earrings two feet long dangling over her shoulders.

2

But Star knew that the audience wasn't that excited just because of the weird outfit. She elbowed her bodyguard, Tank Massimo, who was sitting on her right.

"Tank!" she hissed. "Check it out—that's Capucina!"

"Huh?" Tank blinked and shifted in his seat. He was five and a half feet of solid muscle, and it was obvious just by looking at him that his bulk wasn't ever going to be comfortable in a small folding chair. "What's that, Star-baby? Did you say you're ordering cappuccinos? I could go for that."

Star rolled her eyes, realizing that Tank wasn't even paying attention to the show. "Never mind," she said. "Go back to sleep."

"I wasn't sleeping." Tank sounded slightly wounded. "I never sleep on the job."

"I know, I know." Star giggled, then turned to the woman sitting on her left. "Hey, Lola, did you see? That's Capucina up there!"

Unlike Tank, Star's stylist, Lola LaRue, was watching the fashion show with as much interest as Star herself. Lola was dressed for the occasion in one of Ceasario Pucci's signature hot-pink leather baseball caps. She had even dyed several of her cornrows to match the hat.

"I see her, babydoll," Lola told Star with a smile. "She's even more beautiful in real life, huh?"

"Totally."

"And check out that dress," Lola added with a wink. "Maybe we should get you one of those to wear onstage?"

"Very funny!" Star grinned, imagining how difficult it would be to dance with little plastic spiders bouncing all around her.

She watched with fascination as the supermodel stalked to the end of the catwalk and spun on one spiked heel. Those shoes must have increased her total height to nearly six and a half feet. Being not even five feet tall herself, Star almost felt dizzy staring up at the glamorous creature.

She's just a regular person, like every celebrity, Star reminded herself. Even though she was a celebrity herself now, it was still sometimes hard to remember that. *Of course, she's also a celebrity who happens to be dating Eddie Urbane. . . . I wonder if he's here.*

Squinting against the flashes of the strobe lights, Star glanced around at the rest of the audience. She soon spotted Eddie sitting in the front row on the far side of the catwalk. He was dressed in a stylish dark suit that made him look much older than his seventeen years, and his dark hair was slicked back from his handsome face.

Star watched the young rock star for a moment, though he didn't seem to notice her. It was the first time she'd seen him in person since leaving New York to start her worldwide concert tour a couple of weeks earlier, and she still had mixed feelings about him. She'd been a fan of his for ages; even though he was only three years older than Star, he had been a musical superstar for as long as she could remember. Star had been thrilled when she met him for the first time on an interview show not long before the start of her tour. But she had been less thrilled by Eddie's behavior toward her—especially when she'd discovered his plans to sabotage her tour.

Star bent over again, checking to make sure that Dudley was still under her chair. Of all the sneaky things Eddie had done to her, from canceling her hotel reservations to stealing away some of her background dancers, the sneakiest was dognapping Dudley. Star still had trouble believing that anyone would stoop so low, though Mike Mosley, her manager, had explained that Eddie would do almost anything for publicity. He craved it the same way Dudley craved scrambled eggs or his favorite plastic bone.

When she thought about it that way, Star felt a little sorry for Eddie. She loved performing and enjoyed her life of superstardom—the money, the travel, and everything else. But that still wasn't as important to her as the things that really mattered, like her grandmother, best friend, and other loved ones back home in New Limpet, Pennsylvania, or the ongoing search for her parents and baby brother, who had disappeared almost two years earlier during a vacation in Florida.

Star had already known that Eddie was in Milan and that he might turn up at this fashion show. But seeing him sitting right there across the stage made her suddenly a little nervous about running into him. What would he say to her? What should she say to him?

That stuff he did in New York is all in the past, Star thought, turning back to the stage just as Capucina disappeared behind the curtain with a flourish and a new model appeared to take her place. *If Mom and Dad were here, they would tell me that everyone deserves a second chance. So that's what I'm going to do as far as Eddie Urbane is concerned—wipe the slate clean and start over.*

As the show ended, Star stood up with the rest of the audience to clap. The designer, a tall man with purple hair and a droopy black mustache, stepped out from behind the curtain and began making deep bows in every direction. A moment later all the models started filing back out onstage. Capucina was at the front of the line.

Star noticed that Eddie was standing along with everyone else, but he wasn't applauding. Instead he was staring at Capucina with a hawklike intensity, though the supermodel didn't so much as glance his way.

Weird, Star mused. *I thought they were a couple.*

She was still watching the pair curiously when she heard someone calling her name. A second later Lola elbowed her in the ribs, and Star glanced up to see Ceasario Pucci rushing across the stage toward her.

"Can it be?" the fashion designer exclaimed in a heavy Italian accent. "Is this truly the *bella cantante americana* Star Calloway, at my humble show? *Buona sera, signorina!* It is my deepest honor that you chose to bless us with your presence!"

"Thanks for inviting me," Star said as Ceasario leaned over the edge of the stage and took her hand in both of his. "It was a great show. I really love your clothes—I wore your sparkly tank top in one of my concerts in London."

Ceasario Pucci put one hand over his heart and bowed

slightly. "Ah, you truly do honor me, *signorina*," he said graciously. "Let me return the favor by inviting you backstage. We're having a small gathering to celebrate the show. Please say you and your companions will come as my guests."

At that moment Dudley finally woke up and crawled out from under the chair. He looked up at Ceasario and barked curiously, his curly tail wagging.

The designer laughed. "What a face!" he exclaimed. "Of course, you will bring him along to the party, *si*?"

Star glanced at Tank. "Can we go?" She knew that Mike and the rest of her team were back at the hotel packing, and she had promised to return after the fashion show to help out. But she was excited at the thought of attending her first real fashion party.

Tank checked his watch. "I suppose we could stick around for a little while," he said. "I'm sure Mike and Mags can live without us for an hour or so, right?"

"Yay!" Star exclaimed, clapping her hands with excitement as she turned back to the designer. "Thanks, Mr. Pucci. This should be way fun!"

The designer seemed delighted with her response. "Then please, allow me," he said, hopping off the catwalk and extending his arm. "Perhaps we can even find you a little something else to wear on your tour, hmm?"

Even though Star had been world famous for almost a year, it still felt a little strange to have other famous people want to meet her, hang out with her, and even give her gifts. It wasn't the first time a well-known designer had offered her expensive clothes for free; every time she attended an awards show or other high-profile event, she had her choice of custom-made designer gowns to choose from. As a result, her closets back home were full of one-of-a-kind fashions.

It's weird, she thought, waving to the photographers who were busily snapping pictures of her with Ceasario. *Back when I was just an ordinary kid, there's no way I could've afforded even a sock from these fancy designers' collections. But now that I actually have enough money to buy their clothes, they all want to give them to me for free! How crazy is that?*

Soon she was entering a crowded, smoky, dimly lit room filled with loud talk and even louder laughter. Even in the low light, Star immediately spotted many famous faces—supermodels, actors, and musicians. Thanks to recent lessons with her tutor, Magdalene Nattle, she even recognized a couple of European politicians and at least one member of the

British royal family. Reporters and photographers circulated through the room, seeking out one famous face after another.

Ceasario hurried Star past a cluster of American TV actors who were talking to a reporter near the door. "Come," he said, "let me introduce you to some of my models."

Soon Star, Ceasario, Tank, Lola, and Dudley were surrounded by a small group of models. All of them seemed happy to meet Star, though many of them didn't speak English very well, and Star had a little trouble understanding what they were saying. It didn't help that most of them were at least a foot taller than she was. But she smiled and nodded and did her best to follow the conversation. Fortunately Tank took up most of the slack—Star's bodyguard spoke seventeen languages, which apparently included the native tongues of most of the models.

"Ah!" Ceasario cried a few minutes later, interrupting something one of the models was saying to Tank in what Star was pretty sure was Russian. "Here is the star of my show, *la bellezza di tutte le bellezze*. Wait here, Signorina Calloway."

He lunged into the crowd and returned a moment later with Capucina on his arm. The supermodel had changed out of the spider dress and was now wearing an elegant black pantsuit with beaded cuffs. She looked just as beautiful in person as in photographs, though quite a bit younger; Star estimated that Capucina was no more than eighteen or nineteen years old.

"Here we are, 'Cina," Ceasario said with a flourish. "I want you to meet someone very special."

Just then a photographer appeared. "*Prego,* Ceasario? *Una foto* of you and the lovely ladies?"

"Of course."

Ceasario put one arm around Star's shoulders and the other around Capucina's waist as the photographer snapped several pictures. Star smiled obligingly, glad that Lola had insisted on fluffing up her curly blond hair and straightening her clothes before the fashion show. She certainly didn't want to look anything but her best if she was going to appear in a photo with Capucina!

When the photographer finished, Ceasario continued the introductions as if there had been no interruption. "'Cina, I'm sure you recognize Miss Star Calloway, who has come all the way from the United States to see us. Now, make her feel welcome, *cara mia*—I must mingle." With that he disappeared into the crowd.

"*Ciao.* It is a pleasure to meet you, Miss Calloway," Capucina said in heavily accented but otherwise flawless English. "I am a big fan of your music."

"Thanks," Star replied with a smile. "Please, call me Star. I'm a big fan of yours, too. You were great tonight. I'd like you to meet my driver and bodyguard, Tank Massimo, and my stylist, Lola LaRue."

"It is my pleasure, Mr. Massimo, Ms. LaRue." Capucina's words were polite, but Star couldn't help noticing that she seemed a little distracted. "I would love to chat more with all of you. However, I'm afraid I have pressing business to attend to. Will you please excuse me?"

"Of course," Star said, while Tank and Lola nodded.

"Wonder what that was all about," Tank said, watching as Capucina moved gracefully away until she was swallowed up by the crowd. "Seemed like she couldn't wait to get away from us. Hope it wasn't something I said." He winked at Star, who laughed.

Meanwhile Lola was looking in the other direction. "Hey, I think there's food over there," she said. "Do you guys want anything?"

Before Star or Tank could answer, they heard the sudden sound of shouting. A few yards away, the crowd parted to reveal Eddie Urbane and Capucina facing each other with angry looks on their faces.

"*Silenzio,* Eddie! I will not have you shush me!" Capucina cried, her eyes flashing with rage. She clenched her fist and shook it at him. "I have had enough of you! Get away from me, *per sempre*! We are through!"

"Wait!" Eddie exclaimed, his handsome face flushed. "What are you saying? We need to talk about this. But speak English, for Pete's sake!"

"Aargh!" Capucina threw both hands upward and then launched into a torrent of rapid-fire Italian.

"What's she saying?" Star whispered to Tank.

Tank shook his head sadly. "She's saying that he's a jerk," he translated in a whisper. "That she regrets the day she ever set eyes on his face . . . that she never knew anyone so vain and self-important and immature . . . that his mother was a . . . well, you get the gist."

Star winced. Poor Eddie! One glance at his face told her that he got the gist of what Capucina was saying too, language barrier or not. Even if he and Capucina hadn't been together long, it couldn't feel good to be dumped, especially in front of a bunch of witnesses. To add insult to injury, photographers were now circling the pair, snapping picture after picture. A short distance away, Star noticed Ceasario pushing his way through the crowd, shouting something in Italian. Several large, beefy men who looked like security guards were also making their way toward the couple.

"Come on," Tank said, putting a protective arm around Star's shoulders and glancing at Lola. "Things are getting a little ugly around here. Maybe we should get going."

Star nodded and picked up Dudley, then ducked out through the main door with the others. The mirror-lined hallway outside the party room was silent and completely empty except for a few stray racks of clothes from the fashion show.

"Poor Urbane," Tank said with a rueful laugh. "Talk about public humiliation! This is sure to be in all the papers by morning. First he cancels half his concert tour, and now this. . . ."

Lola shrugged. "Karma," she said succinctly. "It's what that boy deserves for hassling our Star back in New York."

"Guess that's why Capucina seemed distracted when we met her," Star commented. "Maybe she was getting ready to . . ."

Before she could finish the sentence, the door flew open

and Eddie stormed out into the hall. His white tuxedo shirt and his wavy dark hair both looked rumpled, and his face was flushed. He stopped short when he saw Star.

"Oh," he sneered, "it's *you*. I suppose you saw that little scene in there too? It figures."

"I'm sorry, Eddie," Star said sincerely. Despite Eddie's bluster, she guessed that he was really hurt and embarrassed by what had happened. "I really am. You didn't deserve that—nobody does."

Eddie looked surprised. "Oh," he said. "Well, thanks, I guess. Whatever." He shrugged. "It's no big deal. Not like we were that serious, anyway."

As Eddie turned to check out his own reflection in the mirrored wall, Lola nudged Star and gestured toward Dudley, who was sniffing at Eddie's shoes. "Hope Duds mistakes him for a fire hydrant," Lola whispered.

Star bit back a laugh. She knew that Lola still held a grudge against Eddie for what had happened in New York. Dudley seemed to bear his dognapper no ill will, though. After a few more seconds of sniffing, the little dog sat down on Eddie's left shoe and let his tongue loll out happily.

As Star glanced at Eddie, who was straightening his

shirt, she felt another sudden flash of pity. Rock star or not, it was sad to see him standing there all alone, in a foreign city, talking to people he barely knew after being dumped by his girlfriend. Even his usual phalanx of bodyguards seemed to have deserted him for once. It made him seem less like an arrogant, preening superstar and more like a regular kid.

"Hey, Eddie, can we give you a ride somewhere?" Star said impulsively. "We were just going to head back to the hotel anyway. We're at the Ultimo. Where are you staying?"

"No thanks," Eddie said quickly as Lola and Tank turned to stare at Star in disbelief. "I'll just call my . . ."

At that moment the door swung open again. Several reporters and photographers tried to crowd through it all at once, calling out questions to Eddie. One or two of them noticed Star and started yelling questions to her as well.

Eddie glanced at the reporters, then back at Star. "Come to think of it, I could use a ride back to the Ultimo," he said, stepping a little closer until he was standing right next to her. He cleared his throat, his voice getting slightly louder over the cries of the reporters and the clicks and whirs of the cameras. He slung one arm over her shoulders and gave her a hug. "Thanks, Star—you're a good friend."

Star blinked, a little surprised by his sudden change of attitude. "Um, okay." She glanced at Tank. "Shall we?"

Tank nodded and swung into action, holding back the photographers, who were eagerly snapping pictures of the two singers, so he could hustle Star, Eddie, and Lola outside and into the waiting limo.

Two

"So what are you doing here in Milan, Eddie?" Star asked, leaning back against the limo's leather seat.

She immediately winced, realizing too late that she already knew the answer. According to everything she'd read in the papers and seen on TV, Eddie had canceled part of his American tour to fly to Milan to see Capucina.

"Er, I mean, how long will you be in Milan?" Star corrected herself quickly.

"Huh?" Eddie said distractedly. "Oh. I guess I'll probably leave here in the next day or two and go down to Venice. Or maybe I'll just go straight back to Rome—that's where my jet is."

"Really?" Star said. "We're leaving for Rome first thing tomorrow morning. I have some concerts coming up there in a few days."

"Hmm." Eddie didn't seem very interested, and he

returned to his previous occupation of staring out the window at the darkened city streets.

It had been an awkward ride so far. Despite Star's best efforts at making conversation, Eddie had spent most of the ride brooding, except for his occasional bouts of manic chatter, mostly about Capucina's shortcomings.

Still, he's taking the breakup better than I would, Star thought. *If Aaron and I ever broke up . . . Of course, we'd have to actually be going out before that could happen.* She smiled ruefully as she thought about her sort-of boyfriend, Aaron Bickford. The two of them had realized they liked each other shortly before Star got famous. Since then, her career had made it difficult for them to spend much time together.

Noticing that Eddie was still staring out the window, Star searched her mind for something else to say. She shot a glance at Lola, who was sitting across from her in the limo. Lola rolled her eyes at Eddie and stuck out her tongue. Star grinned. Lola was doing her best to be polite to Eddie, but it was obvious she wasn't thrilled to have him in the car. Tank, on the other hand, seemed amused by the whole situation.

It's funny how differently people can react to the same thing, Star mused. *Lola is still so mad about what Eddie did that she* can hardly look at him without growling. Meanwhile Tank just laughs about it—and I know it's not because he cares about me any less than she does. It's just that he's a different person and so he sees it his own way. Sort of like Eddie is totally reacting differently than I would to being dumped in front of half of Milan . . .

"So what's up with that whole Jade thing?" Eddie said abruptly, breaking into Star's thoughts. "With your parents and stuff, I mean. Is that all true?"

Star blinked, startled by the sudden change of topic—for one thing, she was pretty sure it was the first time during the entire ride that Eddie had shown an interest in anything that didn't directly involve him. She saw Tank shoot her a quick, concerned look in the rearview mirror, but he didn't say anything. Star cleared her throat, trying to decide how to answer.

"Don't you think that's sort of an obnoxious question?" Lola said, glaring at Eddie. Her voice was so sharp that even Dudley looked up at her in surprise.

"It's okay, Lola," Star put in quickly. "I don't mind."

Her mind flashed back over the past week. Jade was another teenage American singer who had released her first album a few months earlier. She and Star had met at an awards show in London, and they had spent a few private moments talking about their lives. After Jade had shared a secret about herself, Star had impulsively blurted out her own biggest secret.

"It's true," she told Eddie. "My parents have been missing for almost two years. While I was at an audition in New York, they were on vacation in Florida. One day they took a boat trip and never came back."

"Whoa." Eddie shook his head. "Harsh, man."

"Yeah." Star shrugged. "At first I wished that Jade hadn't told everyone, but now I'm sort of glad she did. It's nice to have it out in the open after all the secrecy."

"Wow." Eddie seemed truly interested in what she was saying for the first time since leaving the party. "Man. They disappeared two years ago? But you've been, like, world famous for almost a year now. How'd you keep the story out of the press all this time?"

"I don't know," Star said. "It wasn't easy. But Mike thought it was important, so . . ."

"Oh, right." Eddie rolled his eyes dramatically. "Figures Mosley would be behind something like that. Seems like his kind of uptight idea."

Star resisted the impulse to leap to Mike's defense. She knew that Mike and Eddie had a history together—or rather, *not* together. Eddie had asked Mike to be his manager about two years earlier, right around the time Mike had first met Star. Eddie had never quite forgiven him for the choice he'd made to represent the up-and-coming Star instead of him.

"Anyway, everyone has been really great about it," Star said, ignoring Eddie's comment about Mike. "My fans and most of the press . . . practically everybody I meet wants me to know they support me, and all kinds of people are logging on to my Web site with tips and stuff. It's great to know that so many people care."

"Uh-huh, sure." Eddie shrugged. "But don't kid yourself. They'll only care as long as you're on top. Then you'll be lucky if your folks rate a question on that *Celebrity Trivia* game show."

"Now, see here, you clueless—," Lola began hotly.

To Star's relief, Tank interrupted to announce that they were approaching the hotel. "And it looks like someone put out the word that we were coming," he added.

Star peered out the window and saw a crowd of paparazzi milling around the entrance to her hotel. The Ultimo was the fanciest hotel in town—most visiting celebrities stayed in one of its many luxurious suites—and there were always at least a few photographers lurking outside, just beyond the reach of the hotel's stern, efficient security guards. But Star had never seen so many paparazzi waiting there before, not even when she'd arrived a few days earlier.

"Yikes," she said. "There are a lot of them tonight."

Eddie leaned past her to look. "Yo," he commented, sounding impressed. Then he leaned back and shrugged. "What a drag."

Beyond the mass of photographers, Star could see other people craning their necks, trying to see. She sighed, wishing that just once the paparazzi would back off a little so her true fans could be at the front of the crowd.

Tank was already on his cell phone calling for backup. A moment later several additional bodyguards appeared and hurried toward the car while hotel security guards cleared a pathway from the curb to the door.

"Too bad my guys aren't here," Eddie commented. "They could clear this whole block in thirty seconds flat. You really ought to talk to your guys, toughen them up a little, Massimo."

"Hmm" was Tank's only response. Star hid a smile.

Star grabbed Dudley and tucked him under her arm. Soon she, Eddie, and Lola were hurrying across the sidewalk, flanked by a muscular wall of guards. Star waved and smiled as dozens of camera flashes went off in a sudden white-hot glare. As tempting as it was to ignore the crowd of photographers that turned up almost everywhere she went, she knew that, as a celebrity, she was expected to look good and act friendly all the time, no matter how tired or disinterested she might really be feeling. It seemed a small price to pay in exchange for all the nice things about her life, and so she did her best to accept it cheerfully even when she wasn't in the mood.

Beside her, she felt Eddie move a little closer. "Gets a little old sometimes, doesn't it?" he murmured in her ear.

She looked up at him and smiled, feeling a sudden flicker of kinship. *He really does know what it's like,* she thought as more flashes went off all around them. *He's been living this a lot longer than I have.*

Before long the hotel staff were holding open the gold-trimmed lobby doors and ushering the group inside. Soon the doors were shut firmly on the crowd outside, and Star breathed out a sigh of relief.

"Home again," she remarked, glancing around the hushed, opulent lobby. As she did, she noticed a very tall man with a shaggy mustache and purple cowboy boots standing near the concierge's desk.

"Mike!" she called, waving. "We're back."

Her manager turned at the sound of his name and returned the wave. He hurried toward Star and the others.

"Howdy," he greeted them in his deep Texas drawl. "I was just talkin' to the desk about our departure tomorr—*oh*. Hello, Urbane," he said, interrupting himself, as he noticed Eddie standing behind Star.

"Mosley." Eddie spat out the name as if it were burning his tongue. "Still doing the cowboy thing, I see?" He nodded disdainfully at Mike's boots.

Mike smiled blandly. "Haven't changed since I saw you three weeks ago."

Eddie scowled. He opened and closed his mouth a couple of times, seemingly searching his mind for another insult.

Tank stepped forward before he could come up with one. "Well, it's getting late," he said with a big yawn that Star was pretty sure was fake. "We'd better get upstairs to bed if we're going to get off in time tomorrow. It's a long drive down to Rome, you know."

"Right. Let's go, y'all." Mike nodded shortly in Eddie's general direction. "'Scuse us, Urbane."

Yikes, Star thought as Mike strode toward the elevator bank at the back of the lobby. *Guess Eddie really does still have some hard feelings about Mike picking me instead of him. Too bad he can't just let it go—it's not as if he's not still a big star even without Mike's help.*

Star glanced back as she stepped onto the elevator. Eddie was slumped against the marble desk, picking at his fingernails. He looked so alone and forlorn that she felt another flash of pity for him.

"I hope Eddie will be all right," she said as the doors closed on her team and the elevator glided upward. She looked up at Mike. "His new girlfriend just dumped him at that fashion show."

"Yeah," Lola put in eagerly. "It was great!"

Star frowned at her. "Come on, Lola," she said. "Don't you feel just a little bit sorry for him? I mean, he had to be feeling all kinds of bummed to actually want to hang out with us."

Mike glanced down at her. "Never mind, darlin'," he said. "I know you mean well, but Urbane doesn't need your help. If there's one thing that boy's good at, it's landing on his feet."

When she stepped into her hotel suite a few minutes later, Star found things in a state of controlled chaos. Suitcases and stacks of paperwork were everywhere, along with boxes overflowing with costumes, clothes hangers, hair dryers, spare microphones, and all the other things that made the group's life on the road flow smoothly.

Star's tutor, known to her as Mrs. Nattle and to everyone else on the team as Mags, looked up from the clipboard she was holding. "You're back." She smiled at Star, pushing her gray hair back from her forehead. "How was the fashion show?"

"It was fun," Star said, stifling a yawn. Grabbing Tank's arm to check his watch, she realized it was almost midnight. "Sorry we're so late. What can I do to help?"

Mike patted the back of a chair. "Plant yourself right here," he told her. "I want to go over your schedule for the next couple of days."

"Okay." Star sat down, pushing aside a stack of Italian newspapers. "Shoot."

As Lola and Tank went to help Mags with the packing, Mike pulled a notebook out of his shirt pocket and straddled another chair. "Okay," he told Star. "As you already know, your first concert in Rome isn't till four nights from now. That means you have a little R and R time. But we do have a few things lined up to keep you busy."

Star nodded. "I know I've got a couple of radio interviews coming up, and that fashion shoot for *Moda*

Costosa magazine is tomorrow afternoon, right?"

"Yep, that's the main reason we have to leave at o'dark thirty tomorrow morning. I want to make sure we get there in plenty of time," Mike said. "I just told the front desk we'll be checking out no later than six a.m."

Star winced at the thought of getting up so early, but nodded. "Okay," she said. "What else is on the schedule for Rome?"

Mike glanced at his notes. "I set up a conference with a couple of your studio's European affiliates, and a TV interview or two, and a short meeting with a local company that wants to turn you into a breakfast cereal or something. And if we're lucky, we might be able to catch up with Lukas Lukas—he's that Swedish film director I told you about last week who's going to be shootin' some footage for your live concert video. He's supposed to have a stopover in Italy in a couple of days, and wants to do lunch to get acquainted before we see him in Sweden next week. Also, you're scheduled to sign CDs at a big new music store opening, and possibly perform a song on a live talk show the night before the first concert, and . . ."

Star listened carefully as Mike reeled off the rest of her upcoming obligations. She was used to having a busy schedule of public appearances and interviews along with her performances. Sometimes it all seemed like too much to fit into a twenty-four-hour day, but somehow, thanks to Mike's careful planning and Star's boundless energy, it almost always all got done.

Finally Mike leaned back in his chair and smiled. "But don't fret, sweetheart," he said. "I built some time into your schedule for fun, too. I know Mags wants to show you a few museums and some of the other ancient historical Roman stuff you've been studyin' with her. And of course there's always your favorite activity. . . ."

"Shopping!" Star finished the sentence for him with a grin. "Sounds fab. I promised Missy I'd try to find her some real Italian sunglasses like in the movies."

"Sounds like a plan," Mike said with a chuckle. "Might as well grab some petty cash now—we haven't packed the pink star yet."

He nodded toward a large, pink, star-shaped wooden box sitting on a table near the suite door. A fan had sent the handmade box to Star almost a year ago, and it made the perfect petty cash container. Mike made sure the star box was always full of cash, so that whenever Star or anyone else on the team needed money—for taxi fares, to tip a delivery person, or just to buy a candy bar at the hotel newsstand or a souvenir at the gift shop—all he or she had to do was grab a few bills out of the box.

Star opened the box and took a fistful of euros. The strange foreign bills still didn't seem quite real to her; she kept expecting to see the more familiar sight of green twenty-dollar bills spilling out of the pink star.

After tucking the money into the small purse where she kept her passport and other important items, which was hanging on the coatrack near the door, she threw herself into the packing chores along with the rest of the team. By the time Mike ordered her to bed an hour later, she could hardly stop yawning.

When she entered her small private bedroom, she saw that someone—probably Lola—had already set out a nightgown, as well as a traveling outfit for her to wear the next day. The rest of her clothes and belongings were already packed in the stack of suitcases and duffel bags by the door—except for her laptop, which was still sitting on the bedside table.

Star knew she should go straight to sleep to prepare for their early departure, but she couldn't resist switching on the computer. She flopped onto the bed and quickly logged on to her biggest fan Web site, which was named after her first album, *Star Power.* As soon as Jade had told the press about Star's missing family, the site's creator, a devoted young American fan named Wendall Wiggins, had created a special page for updates on the ongoing search for the Calloway family. The attached guest book always held new well-wishes and messages from the many fans who visited the site daily.

Quickly scanning through the latest entries on the update page, Star saw that there were no new leads or tips listed since the last time she'd checked. She clicked on the link to the guest book. Noting the hundreds of new entries there, she made a mental note to send Wendall a nice thank-you statement to post on the site. Though she had never given up hope of being reunited with her family someday, it was a little easier to stay strong and optimistic when it seemed that the whole world was cheering her on. Star wanted her fans to know how much she appreciated their support.

But I guess that can wait, she thought sleepily as she logged off and closed the laptop. *Right now I'd better catch some z's, or tomorrow I'll have bags under my eyes so huge that even Lola won't be able to cover them!*

Setting the computer on top of the pile of suitcases so she wouldn't forget it, she changed into her nightgown, fell into bed, and almost immediately dropped off into a sound sleep.

Three

"... and so if the Leaning Tower of Pisa is leaning at an angle of five degrees today, and was leaning at an angle of five-point-six degrees before being stabilized by engineers in 1993, by what percentage was its angle changed?"

Star sighed and tore her gaze away from the gorgeous summer landscape flowing past the tour bus windows to look at her tutor. Mags was sitting across the table from Star in the small but well equipped kitchenette of her tour bus. Star's schoolbooks were spread over the table, but Star had hardly glanced at them in the past hour. There was just too much to look at outside as Tank drove them from Milan to Rome.

"Oh, Mrs. Nattle, how can I think about word problems at a time like this?" Star waved a hand at the scenery. "I mean, just look out there!"

Mags gave her a stern look. "Now, now," she said. "Even pop stars have to learn word problems, you know."

"I know," Star said contritely. She knew better than to argue with Mags when she was in full teacher mode. "Um . . . could you repeat the problem again, please?"

Before Mags could reply, Mike wandered toward them from the tiny office at the back of the bus. He was holding a handful of papers in one hand and his cell phone in the other.

"How's the lesson going?" he asked, swaying slightly back and forth with the motion of the bus.

"Fits and starts," Mags said with another stern look at Star. "Our pupil is bit distracted today."

"'Fraid I need to distract her a little more," Mike said with a rueful smile. "This just came in; thought y'all might like to see. Just pulled it off the Web." Mike set one of the papers he was holding on the table in front of Star. It was a printout of a photograph of Star and Eddie taken the evening before. Eddie had one arm around Star's shoulders and was smiling as he leaned down to whisper into her ear.

"That must've been taken in front of the hotel when we were talking about what a drag the paparazzi can be," Star commented.

Lola, who had been flipping through a magazine in one of the seating areas nearby, wandered over to take a look. "Makes you two look awfully cozy," she commented.

"I guess." Suddenly Star noticed something else about the

photo. "Look! They totally cut Dudley out of the picture!"

Hearing his name, Dudley woke up and looked over at her from his favorite snoozing spot over one of the bus's heating vents. Mike cleared his throat. "I hate to say it, but it seems Lola isn't the only one to think you and Urbane were looking buddy-buddy last night," he said. "And this isn't the only photo they're running to make the point. Check out this one."

He set a second printout on the table. This photo had been taken in the hallway outside the fashion party. Once again, it showed Eddie with his arm around Star.

She blinked. "Oh," she said. "I guess that's right after we offered him a ride. He was just sort of steering me away from the reporters. No biggie." Staring at Eddie's face, which wore a more somber expression in the second photo, she thought back to his spectacular breakup scene. "Poor guy. I wonder what he'll do now that he and Capucina are through. Do you think he has any real friends around to help him through this? He doesn't seem that close with his bodyguards and other staff, and I'd hate to think of him going through something like that all alone."

She couldn't help thinking back to those terrible days,

weeks, and months just after her parents had disappeared. She wasn't sure what she would have done without her caring friends and family helping her through. Her grandmother, Nans; her best friend, Missy Takamori; Mike, Mags, and Tank . . . all of them had made her feel a little less lost, lonely, and confused.

Mags smiled at her understandingly. "It's nice of you to think that way, Star, especially after all the trouble young Eddie has caused you," she said. "But I'm sure he'll be fine."

"No kidding," Lola put in. "That kid goes through famous, beautiful girlfriends like most people go through clean socks. He'll live."

"I guess you're right," Star said, though she still couldn't help remembering the downcast expression on Eddie's face as they'd parted ways in the hotel lobby the night before.

Mike patted her on the shoulder. "Of course they're right," he said lightly. "Now don't spend another New York minute worrying about Eddie Urbane's state of mind—and that's an order."

". . . and then I want to check out the Pantheon, and the Spanish Steps—oh! And Luigi—you know, that Italian sound tech from the studio back in New York?—anyway, he says the Piazza Navona is totally cool, so we definitely have to go there."

Star paused for breath, glancing around eagerly at Mike, Mags, Tank, and Lola. She could hardly believe they were really in Rome. Stepping out of the way of a porter who was lugging the suitcases into their spacious hotel suite, she hurried over and looked out the window just to convince herself that it was real.

From the window, she had a panoramic view of the city. Almost every street corner seemed to feature some kind of architectural wonder dating back to ancient times. After the long ride from Milan, she was ready to get outside, stretch her legs, and explore. Even the throng of reporters, photographers, and fans gathered outside the hotel's front doors immediately below the window couldn't distract her from the sights and sounds of the fascinating city.

Mike joined Star at the window, leaving Tank, Mags, and Lola to finish directing the porters where to put their luggage and equipment. "I was just hopin' to be able to get out of the hotel and find us some grub," he commented, staring down at the paparazzi on the sidewalk below. "But now I'm thinking we'd better stick to room service."

Star's stomach grumbled. When her wake-up call had come at five o'clock that morning, she'd been too tired to eat more than a piece of toast. Lola had fixed them all a snack on the bus halfway through the six-hour drive from Milan, but Star was looking forward to a real meal—and one more bland room-service offering definitely wasn't what she had in mind.

"We can still go out," she told Mike with a touch of impatience. It didn't seem fair that they'd arrived in such a fabulous city and couldn't rush right out and enjoy it. "I'll wear sunglasses and a hat or something. I'm sure we can sneak past those guys. After lunch, maybe we can walk over to the Coliseum or do a little shopping—I don't have to be anywhere until that photo shoot, right? And that's not for, like, three hours."

Mike looked doubtful. "Whoa, let's not get ahead of ourselves," he said. "I suppose we can try to go out to eat. But we're either going to have to get you a better disguise than a hat and sunglasses, or Tank will have to bring along some extra guys. There's been a lot of publicity here about your arrival, and we don't want to take any chances."

"Mike's right," Tank put in, wandering over just in time to hear the last part of Mike's comments. "Rome is a big, busy place. Maybe we should try to—"

At that moment the shrill buzz of one of Mike's cell phones interrupted whatever Tank was about to say.

"'Scuse me," he mumbled, pulling the phone out of his pocket and punching the TALK button. "Mosley here," he said into the tiny receiver, which was half hidden behind his bushy mustache.

He listened for a moment. Star's mind drifted back to the day's plans. Just about the only thing she regretted about her tour so far was that she got to spend so little time in each place she visited. Although Mike had been careful to build in time for sight-seeing, Star was always left wanting more. For one thing, it took her a lot longer to see the sights than it would an ordinary person. By the time she greeted the fans that gathered everywhere she went, waited for her body-guards to clear her a path, and maybe signed a few autographs, it was usually time to go. She wished she had about two weeks to spend in each place. Then she might feel like she was actually getting to see something.

"I see."

Star snapped back to attention. Something had changed in Mike's voice—somehow, those two words seemed to blaze with importance. She focused on his face, trying to read what he was thinking.

Mike didn't meet her gaze. He was staring at a point in space somewhere about three feet above her head. He nodded a few times, obviously listening to whoever was on the other end of the line.

"Okay, then," he said finally. "Keep in touch—you can reach me at this number anytime, day or night. Thanks, Detective Kent."

Star gasped. Detective Kent was the police officer in Florida who was in charge of investigating her parents' disappearance!

"What is it?" she demanded as Mike hung up the phone. She yanked impatiently at his sleeve. "Mike! What did the detective want?"

Mike took a deep breath. He glanced from Star to Tank and then back to Star again. His green eyes were very serious as he finally replied.

"I s'pose you're mature enough to handle this kind of news," he said. "It's nothing definite, you understand. It's just that it's been so long since they've had anything solid to consider, even though this whole Jade business has been bringing wild theories and tip calls and all kinds of crazy hoaxes out of the woodwork . . ."

"What?" Star cried, impatient for once with his usual rambling drawl. "Mike, just spill it already—what did he tell you?"

"Well, like I was sayin', it's nothin' for sure," Mike said. "But the police seem to think they just might've found a clue to the whereabouts of your family."

Four

"What—who—where—did—is—" Star's questions tumbled over each other, trying desperately to escape from her suddenly bewildered brain.

Mike held up a hand to shush her. "Wait," he commanded. "Let's not go all cattywhompus just yet, okay, darlin'? The detective was careful to say that this is just an update, and they're not sure yet that it's not a hoax. He just wants to keep us up to speed, in case—"

"In case they find them soon." Star's eyes were shining as she imagined her most cherished dream coming true at last. "In case it is a real clue, and it leads to the truth, and Mom and Dad and Timmy come home soon. Mike, tell me everything he told you! Please!"

"All right, sweetheart, just give me a chance," Mike replied patiently. "Seems a beachcomber on Banbury Beach found a baby's bib, and—"

"Banbury Beach!" Star interrupted, jumping up and down

with excitement. "That's just a few miles down the coast from where my family left for that boat trip!" In the days and weeks after her parents' disappearances, Star had all but memorized the entire Florida coastline.

Mike nodded. "That's right," he said. "Anyway, like I was sayin', someone picked up this waterlogged bib after high tide last night. Turns out it has your little brother's initials embroidered on it."

Star gasped. "Oh! Mom used to embroider Timmy's and my initials on practically everything—Timmy has all kinds of those bibs! I'm sure he would have been wearing one on the boat!"

"Yep," Mike said. "This beachcomber turned out to be a fan of yours and remembered that from all the news stories that broke after Jade gave away your secret last week. So she turned the bib in to the Florida police right away."

"Wow." Tank shook his head. "That's amazing. If it turns out to be real, it's the first clue they've found in ages."

"Yes," Mike replied. "*If* it turns out to be real. Like I said, they're still not at all sure about that, so let's not get ourselves all in a lather until we hear back from them, okay?"

Star couldn't respond for a moment. She was too over-whelmed with all the thoughts and feelings tumbling around inside her. Could this really be happening?

She touched the silver star pendant she always wore, a gift from her parents not long before their disappearance, and sent a thought of silent thanks to Jade. If it weren't for the other star's big mouth, none of this would be happening. . . .

"Mike," she said at last, still trying to get control of her chaotic, racing thoughts. "How soon can you get me on a plane? I need to get to Florida right away. I need to be there when they find them."

Mike raised one hand. "Whoa, sweetheart," he said. "Let's not get our hopes up prematurely, okay? I understand your feelings, of course, but the timing seems more than a little coincidental. If this turns out to be another hoax—"

"It's not!" Star insisted impatiently. "Come on, Mike. This clue is real; it has to be. I can feel it! And I want to be there when they find my family—I don't want to miss a second of it when they come home." She shivered, already imagining being wrapped in her mother's arms, breathing in the scent of her favorite lavender cologne, feeling her father's kiss on her forehead, and hearing his familiar gentle chuckle. And her little brother, Timmy—he would be almost four years old now! She wondered if he would recognize her. . . .

She was so busy fantasizing about the reunion that it took

her a few seconds to realize that Mike was still shaking his head. "I'm sorry, Star," he said. "I don't think it's a good idea. You have commitments here in Italy, and the investigators don't need you gettin' in their way right now."

"That's a good point," Tank put in. "Not that *you'd* be in the way, Star-baby—but you have to admit that when you show up, you're never the only one. The paparazzi and fans you'd attract would only make the cops' job harder. Besides, it'd be a shame for you to fly all that way only to find out it's a hoax or just a mistake."

"But it's not!" Star exclaimed desperately. Why did Mike and Tank keep blabbing about the bib not being real? Hadn't the detective told them it had Timmy's initials on it? "I want to be there when Mom and Dad and Timmy come home. I *have* to be there!"

"Star, you know I always have your best interests at heart," Mike said calmly. "And lighting out for Florida like the dogs are after you just isn't in your best interests. I'm sorry, but case closed."

Star could tell by the look on her manager's face that his mind was made up. She was so stunned that she wasn't sure she could speak. How could he do this to her?

"Oh," she said, suddenly needing to get away. "Um, I just realized I'm hungrier than I thought. While you guys are deciding about what to do for lunch, I think I'll run down to the lobby and grab some . . . some candy or something."

As the two men exchanged a worried glance, Star whirled around and rushed toward the door, pausing just long enough to grab a few euros from the petty cash box, which Mags had taken out of a duffel bag and set on a table.

Soon she was walking slowly down the quiet, luxuriously appointed hallway of the five-star hotel, her mind tumbling along at a hundred miles per hour. She still couldn't quite believe that the police might be on the verge of finding her family—or that Mike might actually refuse to let her be there when they did.

He'll change his mind, she told herself as she reached the elevator bank. *He has to. He knows how important this is to me—more important than my career, or a few stupid interviews, or anything else in the world. He'll realize that, if I just give him a few minutes to think about it.*

That made her feel better. She pushed a button to call the elevator, and a moment later the polished metal doors slid open, revealing a formally dressed elevator attendant within.

"*Prego*, Miss Calloway," the young man said politely, holding the doors open for her. "Where can I take you?"

"The lobby, please," Star answered, stepping into the elevator.

"Of course."

A few minutes later, Star was wandering across the hushed, plush-carpeted hotel lobby. It felt a little strange to be there all alone; she realized it had been quite a while since she'd been in public without at least one or two members of her entourage at her side. A few other hotel guests were standing near the concierge desk and resting in the overstuffed suede chairs surrounding the gold-plated fountain. One or two people glanced at her curiously when she walked past, but for once nobody approached her or tried to speak to her. That was a relief. Star wasn't sure she was up to making small talk with fans at the moment.

She paused by the small kiosk near the front doors, taking in the shelves full of candy and soda, some exotic, some familiar. But her appetite had deserted her and she had no interest in food. Instead she turned and hurried toward the back of the lobby, where there was a bank of phones.

At least I can get things rolling while Mike figures out how important it is for me to go home, she told herself, reaching for the closest phone.

As she peered at the receiver, trying to figure out how to dial for information, a uniformed hotel employee appeared at her shoulder.

"*Buon giorno,* Signorina Calloway," the young woman said in a lilting accent. "May I be of any assistance to you today?"

"Oh! Thank you," Star said. "I mean, *grazie mille.*" She smiled, pleased to remember one of the phrases Tank had taught her. "I was just trying to figure out how to call the airport. I need a flight to the United States as soon as possible—to Florida, to be specific."

"Of course. Will we be charging it to your suite account, or would you like to use a different credit card?"

"Suite account, I guess." Star hoped that was the right answer. But she didn't worry about it for long; if it was wrong, she was sure Mike could fix it later.

The woman smiled. "Please come with me, and we'll get it all sorted out."

Star smiled back at her with relief, hung up the phone, and followed her toward an office door.

Star was still smiling when she returned to her suite half an hour later. The hotel staff had booked her on the next non-stop flight to Florida. It left Rome at six fifteen that evening—just a little more than five hours away, though even that seemed like a lifetime to Star.

Oh well, at least it will give me plenty of time to pack a few things, she thought as she opened the door and stepped into the suite. *Maybe I'll even be able to help Mike figure out what to do about the interviews and stuff I was supposed to do here over the next few days. . . .*

"Star." Mike's stern voice greeted her just inside the door. "There you are. I was about to send Tank to find you. I just got a very interesting call from the front desk . . . something about booking a car to the airport? I thought you might like to explain just exactly what that's all about."

Star stared up at him, a little startled by the grim expression on his face. "It's okay, Mike," she said. "I was just coming to tell you about that. I figured I'd book myself on the next flight to Florida just to save you some time. There are a bunch of seats left in the first-class cabin; they said it would be no trouble to add Tank to the booking if you want him to come with me."

She glanced at Tank, who was standing a few feet behind

Mike with a serious expression on his normally cheerful face. He shook his head slightly at her, as if warning her not to continue.

But Star knew there was no time to lose. Five hours might seem like a lifetime to her now, but she realized that there was plenty to do in that time. She had no idea how long she would be gone, and she had lots of packing to do and arrangements to make.

"Anyway, I guess I'll just take one bag with me for now until I see what's what over there," she continued. "I'll have to leave Dudley here, of course, but I figured Lola could look after him until I get back, or—"

"Enough!" Mike's voice was low and steady but very, very firm. "Star, perhaps I wasn't clear enough with you before. Exactly what part of 'you're not going' did you not understand?"

Star's jaw dropped. In the two years she'd known him, she had heard Mike use that tone many times—with difficult business partners, annoying paparazzi, and even a rude fan or two. But until now, he had never directed it at her.

"But Mike!" she cried, feeling desperate and angry and a little confused. "You can't—you wouldn't—"

She stopped, unable to continue as she stared into Mike's

resolute green eyes. Could this really be happening? All of a sudden, it was as if Mike were a total stranger who didn't know her at all. How could he act this way? He, more than anyone, should know how important this was to her. If he didn't back down and let her go to Florida, she wasn't sure she could ever forgive him.

Mike sighed and rubbed his mustache. "Look, darlin'," he began. "I'm sorry, but you're going to have to trust me on this one. I know you think I'm being a mean ol' cuss, but I'm just trying to—"

"Never mind," Star interrupted, holding back a sob. "Just forget it." Suddenly she couldn't even stand to be in the same room with him. Not as long as he insisted on acting this way. She had to get away—anywhere. "I—I'm going down to the gym to work out."

Without waiting for an answer, she rushed for the suite door, half blinded by the tears that were spilling over at last.

Five

"Take it easy, Star-baby," Tank said as Star lifted the weight machine with her legs again and again, panting with exertion. "If you do any more reps on that, you'll be too sore to dance at your next show. Why not take a break, have some water or something?"

"Whatever," Star muttered, letting the weights drop and slumping forward on the bench. She wished Tank would leave her alone; the bodyguard had followed her down to the hotel gym, efficiently arranging for the place to be cleared of other guests so that Star could enjoy a rare few moments of privacy during her workout. As in most of the upscale hotels where they stayed, the hotel staff had been happy to comply even on such short notice, closing off the gym and posting several doormen just outside.

I shouldn't take it out on Tank. It's not his fault, Star told herself with a flash of guilt as her bodyguard hurried off to fetch her a bottle of water from a vending machine. *He's not the one who won't let me go.*

She frowned as she thought of Mike, remembering his stern expression as he'd forbidden her to go to Florida. Who did he think he was?

Her legs went to work on the machine again, pumping faster and faster as she thought about their recent conversation. Out of the corner of her eye, she saw Tank set the water bottle on the bench of a nearby exercise machine and shoot her a worried look. But he didn't say anything, instead returning to his post near the door. She felt a wave of gratitude toward him for letting her have her space.

He really cares about me, she reminded herself. *I thought Mike did too. So why would he be so stubborn about this? It's not as if no singer has ever bagged out on a few media stops before. I mean, Eddie Urbane canceled half his American tour to go flying off to his girlfriend's fashion show, and I bet he didn't get all this hassle. . . .*

At that moment she heard the gym door open behind her. She also heard the sudden scrape of metal chair legs against tile floor as her bodyguard leaped to attention.

"Hey," Tank said in a gruff voice. "No one is supposed to be—oh. Never mind."

Curious at his sudden change of tone, Star glanced over just in time to see Eddie Urbane saunter into the room. The young star was dressed in a silky designer track suit over a black T-shirt, with a plush towel slung over his broad shoulders. Several of his hulking bodyguards entered behind him and took up positions near the gym door, ignoring Tank as if he were just another piece of gym equipment.

Eddie sauntered over to Star. "Should have figured you'd be staying here too," he commented as he sat down on the weight machine beside hers, knocking her water bottle onto the floor. "This place is a dump, isn't it? It's not even as nice as the Ultimo back in Milan, and that place was only like half a step above the average loser-snoozer type of place off any interstate back in the U.S. I mean, they don't even have personal trainers for us to use here in the gym!"

Star shrugged, not really in the mood for small talk. "It's okay," she said, ignoring his outrageous comments about the elegant Italian hotels. "Tank's my trainer, anyway."

If Eddie noticed her bad mood, he didn't let on. "Well, isn't he Mr. Multifunctional," he commented. He shrugged the towel off his shoulders and tossed it to the floor, then slid his legs into position and started lifting the weights. "Hey, did you guys drive all the way down here this morning in that bus of yours? That must've taken forever. I just flew in from Milan myself—decided I've had enough of Europe. Too many people speaking foreign languages, not enough ice cubes in the soda. I'm heading back to the good old U.S. of A. tonight. My private jet is at the airport here." He rolled his eyes. "Of course, I was hoping to get out of here sooner than tonight. But the stupid Italian airport people say it'll take, like, hours to get the plane fueled up and ready to go. So I'm stuck here paying for a hotel room I'm not even going to sleep in. And they wouldn't even give me a discount! I swear, the things people do to rip you off if they know you've got money . . ."

He chattered on about himself for a while. Star sat back and stayed quiet, her mind wandering back to her own problems. How was she going to change Mike's mind? Why couldn't he see how important this was to her?

Suddenly Eddie stopped himself in mid-complaint. "Hey," he said, really looking at Star for the first time. "Are you okay? You look kind of weird or something."

Star couldn't help herself. She burst into tears at the thought that even the normally self-centered Eddie seemed more concerned about her feelings than Mike did.

Tank hurried over immediately. "Star, are you okay?" he

said, shooting Eddie a dirty look. "Is Urbane upsetting you?"

"No," Star blurted, trying hard to get control of herself. The last thing she wanted was for Tank to drag her back to the suite. She still wasn't ready to face Mike. "I—I'm fine. Eddie didn't do anything. You can go back over there now."

Tank looked surprised and a little hurt, but he nodded. "Okay," he said. "Just holler if you need me, okay?"

As Tank drifted back to his spot by the door, Eddie raised one eyebrow at Star curiously. "What was that all about?" he asked. "Don't tell me Mr. Musclehead isn't on your best friends list anymore." He jerked his head in Tank's general direction.

Star sighed. "No, Tank doesn't have anything to do with it. It's just Mike who—"

She cut herself off, suddenly realizing that she was about to blurt out the whole story. She bit her lower lip. Wasn't that how she'd gotten herself in trouble with Jade back in London?

Still, look how that turned out, she reminded herself. *If Jade hadn't blabbed, that beachcomber might not have recognized Timmy's bib. . . .*

"Hey." Eddie interrupted her thoughts impatiently. He snapped his fingers in front of her face. "Earth to

Calloway. What's with the dramatic silences and stuff? Don't tell me you're going all dark and brooding like what's-her-name, Jade."

"Sorry," Star said. "I was just—er, never mind. The thing is, I just had a little argument with Mike. He's being really stubborn about something."

Eddie raised one eyebrow. "Oh, really? Mosley, stubborn? I can hardly believe it." His voice practically vibrated with sarcasm. "So what's the problem? He won't let you dye your hair pink?"

Star frowned. "No, it's nothing silly like that," she said. "He won't let me fly to Florida tonight." Before she realized it, she was telling him the whole story.

At the end, Eddie shook his head. "Wow," he said. "Serious stuff. I can't believe that grumpy old cowboy won't let you go back and help look for your folks. Talk about unreasonable."

Normally Star would have jumped to Mike's defense. But this time she remained silent. After all, Mike really *was* being unreasonable. Why shouldn't Eddie point that out?

"So I'm trying to figure out how to change his mind," she said after a moment.

Eddie shrugged. "Why bother?" he said. "I mean, who's the boss in this relationship, anyway? Mike's not the one who has two multi-platinum albums and six number-one singles. He's not the one who's been on the cover of *Teen-O-Rama* magazine more than any other artist in history. Your talent pays his salary, babycakes."

Star was a little surprised that Eddie knew so much about her career, but she didn't waste much time thinking about that.

"I guess that's true," she said slowly, shooting a quick glance at Tank to make sure he wasn't listening to their conversation. "But things aren't really like that with us. We're all a team, you know? Almost like family, really. At least until now . . ."

"Whatever," Eddie said dismissively. "All I know is that it sounds like he's overstepping his bounds, big time. You should just lay the smack down and show Mosley who's in charge. Would do him good to come down a few pegs."

"I don't know," Star said hopelessly. "It's not like I can just up and leave without his okay, right? I mean, I'm only fourteen."

"So what?" Eddie said. "Maybe most fourteen-year-olds couldn't do it. But most fourteen-year-olds aren't headlining their own world tour and pulling down major green. What's he going to do, ground you?"

"I don't know." Star leaned over to pick up the water bottle as an excuse to hide her face. She wasn't sure what to think of what Eddie was saying; it seemed so foreign compared to her life with Mike and the others. Then again, Mike himself was seeming awfully foreign all of a sudden. . . .

As she straightened up and took a gulp of water, Tank wandered toward them. "Everything still okay over here, kids?" he asked blandly, though Star couldn't help noticing the suspicious glance he gave Eddie.

"Yes, we're fine, Tank," Star told him, trying to hide her impatience. "We're just talking."

"Okay." Tank checked his watch. "Might be time to finish up here, though. You still need to eat something before that photo shoot—you and Lola are supposed to leave here pretty soon, and we'll need time to dodge the paparazzi. There was still a whole crowd out front the last time I checked, and for all we know they could be haunting the whole block by now."

"Fine. I'm almost done."

Eddie waited for Tank to leave, then glanced at Star. "Yo, I just had a great idea," he said, lowering his voice slightly. "I know how you can get what you want."

"What do you mean?" Star was distracted, already thinking

about the photo shoot. How was she going to get through it when all she could focus on was that bib in Florida?

"Like I said, I'm heading back to the States tonight," Eddie said. "They tell me the jet will be ready to go by six or so. Why don't you come along?"

Star blinked. "Huh?"

Eddie swung his leg over the side of the exercise machine so that he was facing her. "Fly back to the U.S. with me. I was going to go straight to New York, but hey, Florida sounds fun. I could use some sun."

"Are you serious?" Star shook her head, waiting for the punch line. "You want to fly me to Florida tonight?"

"Sure, it's no big deal," Eddie said. "It's a private jet—there's plenty of room. All you have to do is sneak out and get yourself to the airport around six tonight. You can call Warden Mosley when we're in the air if you're afraid he'll freak out and call the cops or something. By then it'll be too late for him to stop you."

Star held her breath, imagining it. If she accepted Eddie's offer, she could be in Florida before morning!

Then she shook her head. "I can't," she said. "I totally appreciate the offer, but I can't just run off like that."

Eddie shrugged. "Whatever," he said, standing up. "But

think about it, okay? The offer stands." He winked at her and gave his trademark lazy half-smile, the one that made every teenage girl in America swoon. "If you change your mind, just let me know. I'll be over there on the elliptical machine."

Star nodded, too confused to speak. It was a ridiculous plan. She couldn't just skip out, defy Mike's orders, and go to Florida on her own. Or could she?

As Eddie sauntered off toward the other end of the gym, Star leaned back on her exercise bench. Her mind was racing, and her heart was beating faster at the very idea of flying off with Eddie that evening. Normally she would never consider disobeying Mike, no matter how wrong she thought he was or how angry she was with him. But this was so important. . . .

I'd do anything to find my family again—anything, she thought, clenching both hands on the edge of the bench. *Wouldn't I? Yes, of course I would. . . .*

Noticing that Tank was shooting her a curious look from his post near the door, she quickly stood up and moved over to a nearby rowing machine. She sat down and started automatically doing reps, hoping that her active limbs would hide her racing thoughts. She needed to figure this out, to convince herself that there was a better way than Eddie's plan.

But the more she thought about it, the less certain she felt that Eddie's idea was ridiculous. She might be able to convince Mike to change his mind, but it would take time—maybe days. And she definitely didn't want to wait that long. Not when her family could be found at any moment. If she missed that because of Mike's stubbornness, she was sure she would never be able to forgive him. But if she defied him and ran off without even telling him she was going, she suspected that he would never forgive her. And as angry as she was with him at the moment, that second possibility seemed almost as terrible as the first.

If only I had some kind of sign, she thought helplessly, pushing harder than ever on the handles of the rowing machine. *Some kind of clue about what I should do . . .*

She was so lost in her own thoughts that she didn't realize Tank was standing over her until he touched her on the shoulder. "Ready to head upstairs?" he asked. "The photo shoot starts at three, remember?"

"Oh. Right." Star stood up and rubbed her arms, which felt rubbery from exertion. "Three o'clock . . ."

She blinked, realizing that the sign she'd wanted was right

there in front of her. *Three o'clock,* she thought. *That means I should be done by five. Which means I could easily be at the airport by six . . . and with only Lola along, it should be a piece of cake to slip away.*

A thousand possible problems with the plan leaped into her mind. But she pushed them all aside, focusing instead on the image of her family rushing to greet her.

Don't overthink it, she told herself. *Just do it.*

"Okay," Star said to Tank with a slightly nervous smile. Spotting Eddie's towel still lying crumpled on the floor where he'd dropped it, she leaned over and picked it up. "Um, but first I—I want to make sure Eddie doesn't lose his towel. Be right back."

She dashed away from Tank. Eddie was lounging on one of the machines drinking a soda.

Star dropped the towel on his lap. "Here you go," she said. "You dropped this." Glancing around, she lowered her voice. "Listen. I—I'm in. For tonight, I mean."

He looked up at her quickly, his handsome face breaking into a smile. "Really?" he said. "Cool! I thought you'd wimp out for sure. I'll see you at six, then."

"Six," Star repeated, not allowing herself to think too much about what she was planning to do. "See you then."

Six

Star sneaked a glance at the clock on the wall of the dressing room. Three twenty.

"Hold still, dah-ling," the makeup artist said in a thick Italian accent. "You will make me smudge your eyeliner."

"Sorry," Star murmured, trying not to move her lips.

She held back a sigh. It felt as though she'd been in hair and makeup forever. If the shoot didn't get started soon, her plan would never work.

Lola was perched on a stool nearby. "Easy on the liner, Marcella," she told the makeup artist. "Remember, she's only fourteen."

"Of course, dah-ling," the makeup artist said. Pushing back the dozens of bracelets that dangled from her thin, deeply tanned arms, she turned and rummaged in a box of supplies on the narrow white counter behind Star's tall, swiveling chair.

Star looked at herself in the brightly lit mirror that covered most of the wall over the counter. She was wearing a thick terry cloth robe and a pair of flip-flops. So far the makeup artist had lined one of her eyes with purple liner and the other with green. Thick smudges of lavender and lime-green eye shadow swirled upward from her eyelids, over her brows, and almost to her hairline. Her curly blond hair was pulled back for the moment in a tight ponytail; Star could only imagine what the hairstylist would do to it when he returned.

In the background, she could see Dudley sniffing around the base of a metal rack full of outlandish clothes. Usually Star enjoyed fashion shoots—it was like playing dress-up in front of the whole world. But today all she could think about was her plan. Anxiety, guilt, and excitement coursed through her, all at the same time. Could she really pull this off?

"Doing okay, babydoll?" Lola asked her. "You look a little stressed. I hope you're not still mad at Mike—he's only doing what he thinks is best for you, you know."

Star forced a smile. "Sure," she said. "I know."

That was true enough. He probably *did* think his way was best. That was why he wouldn't even listen when Star tried to tell him he was wrong this time. Star couldn't help feeling a flash of anger about that—if only he would be reasonable, she wouldn't have to sneak around and ask Eddie for help.

"I understand how tough this must be for you," Lola went on sympathetically. "Imagining that your parents could be found anytime, wanting to be there . . . But really, you wouldn't be doing the police any favors. Like the guys said, the press would be all over you the second you landed in Florida. They'd only end up getting in the way of the search, you know?"

"That makes sense," Star said carefully as the makeup artist came at her with what appeared to be a tube of black lipstick. She certainly wasn't going to lie to Lola and say she agreed with her. But she also didn't want to give away any hint of her real plans. She had already scoped out the rest of the studio upon their arrival, and she was pretty sure she would be able to slip away when the time came. She shivered slightly as she ran through the plan in her head for the millionth time.

"Please, dah-ling," the makeup artist said. "You must hold still, or I will get this lipstick all over your face and it will look ridiculous."

One glance in the mirror made Star doubt that anyone would be able to tell the difference—in her opinion, her makeup looked pretty ridiculous regardless of where the lipstick ended up. But she did her best to sit still as the woman continued her work.

Finally the makeup artist finished. "All right, dah-ling," she told Star. "You look perfect. Now I will leave you to dress, then Sergio will be in to finish your hair. *Tutto bene?*"

She gestured to a rack of clothing and left the room. Lola was already pulling out a pair of slinky, emerald-green, beaded capris. As Star hopped down from her chair, Dudley barked and raced over to her.

Star bent down and grabbed the little dog. "Okay, Dudster," she told him. "One last hug, and that's it—dog hair won't look very good on the cover of *Moda Costosa.*"

She gave him an extra squeeze before straightening up, feeling bad about using him in her plan and then leaving him behind. But she had already decided there was no other way.

Dudley will forgive me, she told herself as she straightened up. *He's the best kind of friend—totally loyal, no matter what.*

"Ready, Star?" Lola asked, holding out the green pants. "Come on, if we move fast this shoot might actually go off on schedule. Then we can get back to the hotel so you and Mike can work things out."

Star nodded and took the pants from her. She slipped

them on as Lola pulled out a purple silk top decorated with amethysts, emeralds, and peacock feathers.

"Ah, *bellissima,* you look *magnifica!*" the hairstylist crowed as he entered a few minutes later, kissing his fingers enthusiastically in Star's general direction. He held up an industrial-sized bottle of hairspray in his other hand. "Now come, let us take care of the final touches. . . ."

As the photographer conferred with the stylists, trying to decide if they had taken enough film, Star looked up at the nearest clock. Four forty-five.

Cool, Star thought with a quiver of nervous excitement. *I can't believe we're actually finishing early. I just might be able to pull this off!*

Squinting against the bright studio lights, she glanced over at Lola, who was standing on the sidelines with Dudley. She fought back another wave of guilt about what she was planning to do by imagining the happy reunion with her family.

That will make all of this worthwhile, Star told herself firmly, not allowing any hint of doubt. *I'm sure of that.*

As soon as the photographer announced that they were finished, Star thanked him and then scurried back toward the dressing room. She had the green and purple costume half off before Lola got the door closed.

Lola laughed and hurried over to help her. "My, my, you're certainly in a hurry," she said, plucking a few stray feathers out of Star's sleek, upswept hairdo. "Here, let me help you with that—you don't want lose any of those jewels."

"Thanks," Star said, the word muffled as she pulled the feathered top off over her head. "Where are my regular clothes? I have to go to the bathroom."

Lola gestured to a door. "So just grab your robe and duck in there," she said. "We still need to take off your makeup—you don't want to go out on the street like that, do you?"

Star froze, turning to stare at herself in the mirror. She had to admit that she looked ridiculous standing there in her underwear and full makeup.

I forgot about the bathroom in here, she realized, biting her lip and accidentally getting a taste of the thick, gummy black lipstick. Her heart pounded at the thought that her whole plan might be falling apart before it began.

"Um—never mind," she told Lola quickly. "I can wait. Come on, let's get this gunk off my face."

"You sure?" Lola said. At Star's nod, she shrugged. "Okay, plant yourself. This could take a few minutes."

She went to work, scrubbing most of the eye shadow, lipstick, and foundation off Star's face. Finally all that was left was the eyeliner.

"Hmm," Lola commented, dabbing at it with a makeup sponge. "This stuff isn't coming off very easily. Hold on, I can probably find something that will get it—"

"Never mind," Star blurted, noticing that the clock on the wall now read five o'clock. She leaped out of the makeup chair, grabbing her street clothes and rapidly pulling them on as she spoke. "We can get that when we go back to the hotel. First, I think Dudley needs to go out. Would you mind taking him? I still need to go to the bathroom myself. But, um, the one in here smells a little funny. I think I saw one out in the hall behind the main studio—I'll go try that one instead."

Lola looked startled by Star's sudden burst of energy. But she shrugged. "Okay, babydoll," she said. "Whatever you say. I'll meet you by the front door in a few minutes, okay? Tank should be here to pick us up by then." She whistled for Dudley, pulling his leash out of her jacket pocket. "Come on, Mr. Do-Wrong. Potty-break time."

Star watched as Lola snapped the lead onto Dudley's collar, fighting back the urge to rush forward and give them both a hug. How long would it be until she saw them again?

Not as long as it's been since I've seen Mom and Dad and Timmy, she reminded herself.

That gave her the extra strength she needed. As soon as Lola and Dudley disappeared down the hall toward the front door, Star headed the other way. She picked up speed as she darted past the door to the studio, heading toward the back of the building. A squeak of surprise escaped her as she rounded the corner and almost ran headlong into the hairstylist from the photo shoot.

"Signorina!" the man exclaimed. "Can I help you with something, *cara mia?*"

"N-no," Star blurted out nervously. "Um, thanks anyway. I'm fine. Just need a bathroom break, that's all. No biggie."

She brushed past the stylist, almost running as she headed down the hallway and dashed into the women's room. For a moment she just stood there leaning against the door, trembling from head to foot.

"Pull yourself together, Calloway," she muttered aloud. "You can do this."

Taking a deep breath, she peered out into the hall. The hairstylist had disappeared, and there was no one else in sight.

Star checked her jeans pocket, feeling for the thick wad of euros she'd taken from the petty cash box on her way out of the hotel. In her purse were directions to the airport and to the police station in Florida, as well as her passport. Her handheld computer was in her jacket pocket, along with a pair of sunglasses and a few other items she'd thought she might need.

I'm as ready as I'm ever going to be, Star told herself. *So let's go!*

Not allowing herself any further hesitation, she dashed down the hall toward the rear exit door leading to the street.

☆ ☆ ☆ ☆ ☆

From: singingstar01

To: MissTaka

Subject: Update on THE PLAN

Hey Missy,

OK, I made it 2 the airport! I just hope I'm in time. It's 6 on the nose & EU isn't here!!! I hope he doesn't flake on me or I don't know what I'll do!!!!! Can u believe I'm really doing this??????

4 a while I didn't think I'd make it here at all. Do u know how hard it is 2 find a taxi in Rome??? Especially when u're trying not 2 B seen . . . NEway, I finally flagged 1 down, & luckily the driver was some grumpy old dude who didn't recognize me. Or maybe not so lucky—the ride cost so much that I'm almost out of euros already!!! Who knew taxis were so $$$?

I almost got caught when I got here, 2. A couple of peeps spotted me, but I convinced them it wasn't me. (My hair still looks weird from the shoot—all slicked back & stuff.) I bought a hat in the airport gift shop w/most of the rest of my $$ and also a pair of ugly reading glasses that make my eyes look tiny. I guess it helps that I'm by myself, 2—makes it easier 2 slip past everyι.

OK, better go look 4 Eddie again—I hope I'm in the right meeting place!!!

More l8r . . .

Yr nervous bff,

Star

Star punched SEND and stuck the handheld back in her pocket. Writing to Missy had distracted her a little, but she was growing increasingly nervous with every passing second.

Where the heck is Eddie? she wondered, peering around over the top of her glasses. She knew it was only a matter of time before Mike and the others figured out where she was. *He'd better get here soon, or this whole plan will go up in flames. . . .*

Suddenly she heard a familiar voice shouting, accompanied by the sound of running feet. She shrank behind a pillar, pulling her hat farther down over her face. Then she peered out carefully.

"Mi scusi! Mi scusi!"

A second later Tank sprinted into view, his broad face red

with exertion. Mike was right behind him, along with a frantic-looking Lola. Several airport security guards were jogging along behind them, looking slightly confused. Behind the guards were a handful of paparazzi, holding their cameras at the ready and staring around the airport eagerly.

"Star?" Lola cried at the top of her lungs. "Star Calloway! Where are you? Please come out!"

Star pressed herself against the scratchy cement of the pillar, her heart pounding. Now what?

For a second she was tempted to step out and turn herself in. Just looking at Lola's sobbing face and hearing the anxious crack in Tank's voice made her feel mean and small inside. She hated to make them worry so much. Besides, maybe they had realized how serious she was about this; maybe now they would be willing to let her go.

Or maybe not. She couldn't take that chance. Not with so much at stake.

As an image of her family flashed through her head, she squeezed herself farther behind the pillar, forcing herself to keep still. Could she still do it? Even if Eddie showed up, would she be able to sneak past the people who were looking for her? A curious crowd was already gathering around her team. Soon everyone in the airport would be looking for her, and her unusual hairdo and weird glasses weren't likely to stop them this time.

Just then she heard Mike's voice shouting something about a certain gate number. Star gasped, realizing that the adults must think she was still trying to get onto the commercial flight she'd booked earlier. She peeked out cautiously once again, just in time to see the whole group sprint off toward the other end of the terminal.

All right! she thought, swallowing back the thick wad of guilt that seemed to be taking up residence in her throat. *Now, if Eddie ever shows up, maybe we can get this show on the road.*

A moment later she breathed out a sigh of relief as she finally spotted Eddie striding through the airport with a large group of muscular bodyguards behind him. Several fans rushed up to him eagerly, but Eddie walked past them as if they didn't exist, leaving his guards to brush them off.

Star glanced around quickly to make sure her people were nowhere in sight. Then she dashed across the open floor toward Eddie's group as fast as she could.

"Yikes!" she exclaimed as she reached them. "I'm glad you're here. They almost spotted me just now!"

"Who?" Eddie asked, glancing around the airport. He ran one hand over his sleek dark hair and wet his lips. "The press? Where?"

Star shook her head, panting. "No, no—Mike and Tank and the others. They're here! If they see me . . ."

"Oh! Got it." Eddie snapped his fingers at his bodyguards. The large men moved quickly, surrounding Star and Eddie with their massive bodies. One of them shrugged off his dark trench coat and wrapped it around Star.

Star went limp with relief. She allowed Eddie to take her arm and steer her along, encircled by the wall of bodyguards.

"It's all right, don't worry," Eddie told her. "We've got you now. We'll be in the air in no time."

"Thanks," Star said quietly, trying not to think about what her team might be thinking and feeling when they discovered she wasn't on the other flight.

"So I guess this means Mosley didn't come around?" Eddie asked cheerfully. "Told you he was hopeless."

Star shook her head, feeling a combination of anger and guilt. "There wasn't enough time to convince him," she said quietly, trying not to recall the anxious look on Mike's face as he'd run past her just now. She touched the handheld in her pocket. "Will I be able to send e-mails from your plane? Or make a phone call, at least?"

"Sure," Eddie replied proudly. "My plane has all the latest tech. Each seat has its own private media system built right in, including a TV and a computer with online access and video games and stuff. You won't be able to use your own computer to e-mail in the air, if that's what you mean, but yeah, you can send e-mail. Or call, whichever."

"Good. Thanks." Star was relieved. Once she was safely on her way, she planned to notify her team about where she was. That way they wouldn't have to worry about her any longer than necessary.

"Please prepare for takeoff, Miss Calloway." A pretty, soft-spoken flight attendant smiled and leaned over to check on Star's seat belt. "Once we're airborne, I'll be back to offer you some refreshments."

Star returned the young woman's smile. "Thank you."

Turning away, Star glanced around the interior of the plane. Eddie had outfitted his jet with every possible luxury. The back of the plane, where she, Eddie, and the bodyguards were sitting, held several rows of wide, comfortable seats covered in black-and-white pony-print suede. Each seat also had Eddie's name stitched on it in gold thread, and the clasps of the seat belts were studded with real onyx and pearl.

The rest of the plane looked like a particularly opulent game room. The floor was covered in plush carpeting, and framed gold records and real oil paintings—many of them portraits of Eddie himself—hung between the windows on the side walls. There were several comfortable black leather sofas and overstuffed chairs scattered around, along with a full-size pool table, a blackjack table, a couple of pinball machines and other video games, and even a roomy Jacuzzi. A huge entertainment center took up most of the front area of the plane, and each chair and sofa had a small TV screen on an adjustable swivel stand coming out of its side and a speaker embedded in its arm. A full kitchen was tucked into the very back of the plane behind the seats, complete with a stainless-steel refrigerator and a cappuccino machine. The whole plane made Star's comfortable tour bus seem like a stripped-down school bus in comparison.

Normally Star might have enjoyed a trip in such extravagant surroundings. But at the moment, all she could think about was where she was going.

I'm coming, Mom and Dad, she thought, closing her eyes as she felt the plane begin to taxi down the runway and pick up speed. *I'm coming.*

Seven

From: MissTaka

To: singingstar0l

Subject: R U here yet????

Hey Star,

Just checking in b4 bed 2 C where u r now. I can't believe ur really flying back 2 the US in EU's private jet!!! And I TOTALLY can't believe ur family might b back so soon!!!!!!!!!!!!! U have to let me know as soon as u find out more, OK? (I know u will!)

NEway, don't worry 2 much about Mike. U gotta do what u gotta do. He shouldn't have tried 2 stop u. He might b mad now, but he'll get over it when he Cs how happy u r when ur family is back!

Write back when u can!

Love,

Missy

Star peered out the airplane window, trying to figure out whether she had time to answer her friend's e-mail. Below, dazzling pinpoint lights appeared to tilt wildly back and forth as the jet circled the airport in preparation for landing. It was almost ten p.m. Florida time, and the last few traces of pink and gold were fading into velvety darkness on the western horizon.

"Please prepare for landing," the pilot said over the speaker system. "We should be on the ground in twenty minutes."

"Finally!" Eddie exclaimed, looking up from one of the pinball machines. "I thought this stupid flight would never end. Why does Europe have to be so freaking far away, anyhow?"

Star stifled a yawn, turned off the computer at her seat, and reached down to fasten her seat belt. It was almost four in the morning back in Rome, and she was tired. Spending so much time on the road had taught her to catch naps whenever she could, but it had been hard to get much sleep on the plane. She had started the flight trading e-mail messages with her team. She'd considered calling them instead, but e-mail was safer. She wasn't ready to hear their voices just yet.

Lola and Tank had written back to her right away, both of them sounding more relieved that she was all right than angry about what she'd done. Mags had returned her message promptly as well, scolding her soundly but also mentioning that both she and Mike were relieved that she was safe. Mike himself had not responded, though she'd sent him several e-mails trying to explain why she'd done what she'd done.

Guess that means he's really mad, Star thought as she watched the city lights move closer. Her fingers tightened on the arms of the leather airplane seat, and she scowled at her own reflection in the small window. *She* was the one who should be mad, not him. If he'd just let her go in the first place . . .

She yawned again. Even after she'd given up on hearing from Mike, an hour or two into the flight, she still hadn't been able to get much sleep. First Eddie had challenged her to a game of pool, then spent the whole time they were playing talking about his favorite subject—himself. At first Star was happy to discuss any topic that might distract her from her own problems for a while. But eventually it got boring listening to Eddie blab on and on about his latest album, his latest video, his tour, his cars and homes and expensive toys, and all the rest of it.

Later she'd managed to curl up on one of the sofas and drift off for a while. But she had only been asleep for a few hours when Eddie had decided to pull out an electric guitar and break into a one-person, extra-loud jam session.

Star was grateful to Eddie for offering to help her, for going out of his way to fly her to Florida. But she had to admit that she wouldn't be sorry to part ways with him once they landed.

As she glanced out the window again to check on their progress, the same soft-spoken flight attendant approached her seat. "Excuse me," she said. "Please fasten your seat belt to prepare for landing, Miss Calloway."

"Thanks, Susan. It's already fastened." Star smiled up at the woman. "And thanks again for everything. That omelette you made me was really good."

The attendant blushed slightly. "You're quite welcome. It was a pleasure to meet you, Miss Calloway."

"I told you, please call me Star," Star insisted.

Susan smiled. "All right—Star," she said. "Now if you'll excuse me, I need to check on Mr. Urbane."

Star settled back against her seat as the plane dipped lower. She closed her eyes, counting the seconds until they were on the ground and she could get on with her mission.

"Uh oh," Eddie said. "Heads up—looks like some photographers found us."

Star glanced up and saw a small group of paparazzi rushing toward them through the almost empty main hall of the airport. She expected Eddie to signal for his bodyguards to fend them off, as the guards had done with the curious onlookers who had noticed them when they were exiting the plane and going through customs. Instead, he flung one arm around her shoulders and grinned as the paparazzi rushed up to them.

"All right, all right, boys," he sang out. "Just a few shots. Star and I have places to be; we can't hang around here with you losers all night."

Star forced herself to smile as the photographers circled them, eagerly snapping picture after picture. She was so tired that she could hardly keep her eyes open, and she wished she'd remembered to touch up her makeup before landing. If she showed up in the press looking as haggard as she felt, she knew that Lola would be horrified.

At least I managed to scrub off most of that weird eyeliner in the plane bathroom, Star told herself, automatically forcing her eyes wide open despite the flashes' glare. *And my hair is mostly back to normal.*

She'd been pleased to discover that the bathroom on Eddie's plane was as well equipped and luxurious as the rest of it. She'd washed her hair in the gold-fixtured sink, dried it with the industrial-strength blow-dryer, and removed the last of the makeup from the fashion shoot with the help of the fully mirrored wall behind the marble sink and a large tub of cold cream she'd found in the mahogany cabinet.

As her tired mind drifted, she gradually became aware that the paparazzi were shouting questions as they snapped pictures.

"What are you two doing here together?" one man called out.

Another photographer elbowed the first one in the ribs, trying to get closer. "Star! Does this mean you're giving up on your tour?"

"Eddie! Eddie!" yet another photographer yelled. "How long have you and Star known each other? Where did you meet?"

"No comment," Eddie called out. "Just get your shots and then leave us in peace, okay? My good friend Star and I have lives to live here, and we'd appreciate some privacy."

In the end, it took a few menacing words from Eddie's beefy bodyguards to clear a path through the paparazzi. After dodging a few more photographers and fans, they found themselves in a quiet spot in a hallway.

"Okay, then," Eddie said abruptly. "Guess this is good-bye."

Star blinked, surprised. "Oh," she said. "Um, all right. Thanks again for the ride. I really appreciate it—I owe you one, Eddie."

"Whatever." Eddie shrugged and checked his watch, seemingly disinterested in the whole conversation. He glanced at his head bodyguard. "Yo, Rochester," he said. "How long will it take to refuel? I want to get back to New York sometime tonight."

"I'll check on that for you, boss," the bodyguard replied, already moving away. He paused long enough to glance at Star with concern in his dark eyes. "Uh, but what about her? Shouldn't we, like, make sure she gets where she's going? I mean, we can't just leave her here, right? It's nighttime and all, and she's just a kid."

"Yeah," one of the other bodyguards put in, cracking his knuckles anxiously. "I was just thinking the same thing."

Eddie scowled at them. "Hey," he snapped. "I don't pay you guys to think, all right?" He jerked his head toward Star. "And *she* doesn't pay you at all, so quit whining about her like a bunch of girls. Now move! I need to make a few calls before we leave."

The bodyguards exchanged a glance and a shrug. As

Rochester continued off on his errand, Eddie and the rest of the men turned to follow.

Eddie cast one last glance over his shoulder at Star. "See you," he called. "Oh, and good luck with that parent thing."

"Thanks."

A moment later Eddie's group turned the corner, leaving Star standing in the hallway by herself. She glanced around, suddenly feeling very alone. Now what was she supposed to do? She realized she wasn't used to being on her own. She was accustomed to having Mike or someone else on her team standing by at all times to direct her, to organize her life and make sure she was where she was supposed to be at all times.

Have I really become that helpless? she wondered uneasily. *How lame is that? I mean, before I got famous I wouldn't have thought twice about doing stuff on my own—and I was just a kid then!*

That thought gave her the extra motivation she needed to snap out of her momentary helplessness and confusion. She looked around again and caught a glimpse of her own reflection in a mirrored pillar nearby.

She gulped. Now that Eddie's bodyguards were gone, she'd better get incognito—and fast. But how? She reached into her pocket and fingered her few remaining euros. They wouldn't last her long. She'd have to change them into dollars, and after that she wasn't sure they would even pay for a taxi into town, let alone buy her a serviceable disguise.

Hearing footsteps approaching from one end of the hall, she darted off the other way. Turning the corner, she saw that she had just come upon the main shopping area of the airport. It was late enough by then that many of the shops and restaurants were closed, their entrances blocked off by iron grilles. But a few places were still open, including a nearby bookstore.

She decided she'd better get out of sight while she figured out a plan. Otherwise, those paparazzi were likely to turn up and trap her. She'd never had to deal with them without Tank or other bodyguards before, and the thought scared her more than she would have expected.

As she stepped into the bookstore, she saw with relief that it was completely empty of customers. She also noticed that one of her own songs, "Never Give Up," was playing softly on the store's sound system. She smiled slightly, humming along with the lyrics: "Never give up, you'll get there someday / Never lose hope, you'll find a way. . . ." After singing the song onstage so many times in the past few weeks, the words were so familiar that she hardly ever thought about them anymore. Suddenly, though, they seemed to take on special meaning.

I can't give up, she thought. *That's why I'm here, right? It's silly to waste time being scared when I have important things to do.*

Suddenly she heard a gasp from behind the counter.

"Star! Star Calloway! No way! Is that really you?"

Star turned and saw a teenage girl standing behind the counter. The salesgirl had a magazine in her hand and an astonished expression on her face. She stared up at the sound-system speaker above the counter, which was still playing Star's song, then back at Star again.

"Hi there," Star said. "Yes, it's me. Um, I could use some help, actually."

The girl dropped her magazine and hurried around the counter. "Sure!" she exclaimed, tugging on her long, black braid. "I'll do anything you need, Star. It would be a total honor."

"Is there somewhere we could talk in private?" Star glanced anxiously over her shoulder toward the airport aisle just outside. "You know—out of sight."

"Sure thing." The girl gestured for Star to follow her toward a door behind the counter. "Come this way. I haven't had a customer in twenty minutes at least, so I'm sure nobody will bother us in here."

"Great." Star's expression relaxed slightly into a more sincere smile. She followed the girl through the door into a storage room. "What's your name?"

"Tracy," the girl replied. "I'm, like, your biggest fan. In fact, I was just reading a story about you in a magazine. Is it true that you and Jade made up and are the best of buds again?"

"Um, sort of."

"Cool!" Tracy said. "'Cause you two are my total heroes. I want to be a singer too—I'm just working here for the summer." She waved a hand at the bookstore. "Also, my parents are going to make me go to college before I try to break into the music business. Do you think that's a mistake?"

"Uh . . . I'm not sure. My tutor always says that even pop stars need to learn stuff. I think she's probably right—she usually is." Star took a deep breath, wondering how to explain her predicament. "Look, Tracy, I'm sort of in a jam. I need to get to the police station in town, but I don't have much cash on me, and my bodyguard and manager aren't here, and I'm afraid if I step outside I'll get totally mobbed by photographers and stuff. I need, like, a disguise or something."

Tracy held up a hand. "Say no more," she said, sounding delighted. "I'm on it."

Star blinked in surprise as the salesgirl rushed out of the storeroom. Then she sat down on a box of cookbooks to wait. She reached into her pocket, touching her handheld computer and wondering if she should try to e-mail Mike again. It was almost five o'clock in the morning back in Rome, but she suspected he might still be awake.

He probably wouldn't answer this one, either, she decided, her stomach twisting nervously at the thought. She pulled her hand out of her pocket and raised it to her throat, touching her star necklace for comfort.

"She's in here," a voice sang out from just outside the storeroom.

A moment later, Tracy rushed back into the small room, followed by two other girls around her age.

Star stood up quickly. "Hey," she said. "I—I thought you were going to find me a disguise, Tracy." *Not just bring all your friends around to gawk at me,* she added to herself, though she didn't say it out loud.

Tracy smiled brightly. "No worries," she said. "Just bringing in some reinforcements. Kait works in one of the clothing stores down the aisle, and Alanna here is an assistant manager at the Accessory Shoppe. Check this out—we've got the perfect disguise for you!"

Star noticed with relief that each of the newcomers was carrying a shopping bag. *Whew!* she thought. *Guess lack of sleep is making me grumpy and suspicious.*

"Cool," she told the three girls sincerely. "Thanks a million. Let's see it!"

Fifteen minutes later, Star peered cautiously out into the airport aisle. It was almost eleven o'clock at night, and there were only a few passengers hurrying back and forth, most of them too busy with their own errands to glance toward the small group in the bookstore entrance.

Star took a deep breath and glanced back at Tracy, Kait, and Alanna. Kait gave her a thumbs-up.

"You look awesome," she said. Then she giggled. "Okay, maybe awesome isn't the right word. You look, um . . ."

"Very convincing," Alanna supplied helpfully.

Tracy nodded and grinned. "Trust us," she said. "You're going to fit right in here in Florida."

Star smiled and glanced at her reflection in one of the airport's mirrored pillars. She was sure that even Lola would have to admit that her new friends had done a fantastic job.

They had dressed Star in a shapeless polyester dress that reached past her knees, a baggy sweater, and saggy tights. A scarf topped with a floppy sun hat covered her bright blond hair, and large tinted glasses hid half her face. Finishing out the costume were a pair of beige orthopedic shoes and a cane. Star's own clothes were tucked into the shopping bag she carried in the hand that wasn't holding the cane. Even Star hardly recognized herself in the mirror. Her petite frame and pretty face had been totally transformed by the change of clothes. She looked just like a little old lady!

"Okay, slump a little," Kait instructed. "Lean on the cane and make sure to walk slowly."

"Got it." Star took a few practice steps, hunching as much as she could. She grinned, imagining what her dance coach and choreographer would say if they could see her now.

"Excellent!" Tracy exclaimed. "You're, like, a natural actress. That reminds me. How come you haven't been in any movies yet? I heard Jade is already signed on to play the villain in the next *Hero McSpy* sequel."

Star shrugged. "Really? I didn't know that." She wasn't really in the mood to discuss her career strategies at the moment, but she didn't want to be rude, especially after the girls had helped her so much. She decided to change the subject. "Listen, you guys are so awesome! I really don't know what I would've done without you. I swear, I'll send you money to pay you back just as soon as I get in touch with my team tomorrow, okay?"

"Sure, no hurry," Kait said, and the others nodded.

Star pulled out her handheld, quickly checking to make sure she had the three girls' addresses. Not only had they put the clothes they'd used for her costume on their store charge accounts, but they had all chipped in to provide Star with enough cash to get into town. She definitely didn't want to stick them with her bill.

"Maybe we'll see you when you come to town for the American part of your tour," Tracy said shyly. "We already made plans to go sleep out for tickets."

"Really?" Star said. "No need to do that. I'll send you guys front-row seats." As the girls gasped and blurted out their thanks, Star made another note on her handheld to remind herself of her promise. "Don't thank me—you totally earned them," she said with a grin. "It's the least I can do!"

Then she tucked the little computer into her shopping bag and checked her watch. Now that her disguise was finished, her impatience was returning. She could hardly wait to get to the police station and find out what was happening with the investigation. What if they'd already checked out the bib and started the search for her family? What if they'd already found them, and her parents and baby brother were waiting for her at the station right now?

Star shivered with excitement. "Okay," she said briskly, taking a few quick steps out into the aisle. "Here I go!"

"Slower!" Tracy reminded her. "Little old lady, remember?"

"Oops." Star quickly adjusted her position. "Thanks again for everything. Anyway, I'd better get moving before it gets any later. Um . . ."

Glancing up and down the aisle, she realized she had no idea where to go. Until that day, she had never taken a taxi that someone else hadn't hailed for her—Tank, or Mike, or before them, her parents. She'd managed to do all right back in Rome, but she had no idea how to go about finding a cab.

The older girls exchanged a glance. "Can one of you take her?" Tracy asked the others. "I wish I could go, but my dad is supposed to pick me up in like five minutes and he'll freak if I'm not at the store."

"Oh, don't get in trouble on my account!" Star said quickly. "I'm sure I can figure it out."

"Don't worry," Alanna said. "I've got some time left on my break. Come on, Star—this way."

"Thanks." Star had to admit she was relieved not to be left alone just yet.

She followed as Alanna led the way out of the shopping area and down an escalator. There were more people on the airport's lower level, but no one so much as glanced in Star's direction. She wasn't sure which felt stranger, shuffling along at a snail's pace, or walking through a busy airport unnoticed. She even walked right past a small cluster of photographers without earning so much as a glance from them, even though she recognized one or two from the group that had surrounded her and Eddie earlier. Part of her was relieved to be able to creep right past them without having to stop and smile and pose and answer questions, but another part of her was surprised at how strange it felt. It had been a long time since she was just part of the crowd.

Finally they stepped out through a pair of automatic doors into the warm night air, made stale and stifling by the cement parking garage overhead. The taxi stand was just outside the doors. Several cars were waiting for customers, and the attendant pointed toward the one at the front of the line.

"Right this way, ma'am," he said, taking her by the arm and guiding her along.

Star bit back a giggle. Not daring to answer, she simply nodded.

"Thanks," Alanna answered for her. As Star climbed into the backseat, the older girl leaned in the front window. "My grandmother needs to go into town." She gave the driver the address of the police station. Then she winked at Star. "So long, Granny."

Star smiled and waved, still not daring to speak. If the taxi driver happened to recognize her voice, it could be a disaster.

Luckily, the driver didn't seem interested in talking. Mumbling something about how long the ride would take, he steered away from the curb and headed down a ramp toward the highway.

Star leaned back against the ripped, lumpy seat and sighed. Soon. Soon she would have the answers she needed.

Eight

Star stepped into the police station and looked around. It was nearly midnight, but it might as well have been the middle of the day judging by the level of activity. Behind a large desk, several officers were filling out paperwork or talking on the phone. A row of chairs against one wall held a variety of people, including a tired-looking mime and a very fat young man wearing nothing but handcuffs and a stained toga. Through several open doors leading into the back of the station, Star could see other officers rushing back and forth.

She stepped up to the desk and waited until one of the officers, an older woman with short salt-and-pepper hair, hung up the phone and glanced up at her. She reminded Star a little of Mags, which made her feel slightly more confident.

"Excuse me," Star said. "Um, is Detective Kent here? I really need to talk to him."

The officer shrugged and returned her attention to the

phone, dialing so quickly that her fingers were little more than a blur. "Have a seat, ma'am," she told Star in a bored voice. "Someone will be with you in a little while."

Star bit her lip and glanced at the row of chairs. Not knowing what else to do, she perched on the edge of an empty seat beside the mime. Glancing around, she realized she was the youngest person in the room, even though she still looked like one of the oldest.

The young man in the toga leaned over the mime and stared at her. "Hey," he said loudly. "You look just like my grandma. Grams? Is that you?"

"Sorry, you have the wrong granny," Star replied.

The toga guy blinked. "Oh, well," he said sadly. "I was hoping you were here to bail me out."

Star sighed and leaned back in the hard wooden chair. Once the toga guy lost interest, nobody else paid her the slightest bit of attention. Even the officers behind the desk seemed to have forgotten all about her. Ten minutes passed, then fifteen.

It's like I'm invisible, Star thought in frustration after glancing up at the clock over the desk for about the millionth time. *Maybe they're just hoping I'll go away and they won't have to deal with me. . . .*

Finally, after another ten minutes passed, she couldn't stand it anymore. She needed to get some attention, and luckily she knew exactly how to do it. Standing up, she unbuttoned her cardigan sweater and shrugged it off. Then she removed her glasses and pulled off her floppy hat and the scarf underneath, shaking out her trademark blond curls.

The toga guy leaned forward again curiously. He gasped. "Hey, check it out!" he exclaimed. "My grandmother just turned into that girl singer from PopTV!"

"Whoa," the mime said, then clapped a hand over his own mouth.

Star stepped toward the desk, leaving the pieces of her disguise behind on the chairs. "Excuse me," she said firmly. "I'm Star Calloway, and I'm here to see Detective Kent. I was just wondering if he's available yet?"

The first woman was still busy on the phone, but a couple of other officers gaped at Star in amazement. "Star Calloway," one of them said. "Hey, my kids love you!"

"Hold on, Miss Calloway." The second officer was already heading for a door at the back of the room. "Let me tell Kent you're here."

A few minutes later Star was sitting in a small, messy office in the back area of the station. Sitting across from her at a battered metal desk was Detective Kent, the offi-cer in charge of her case. He was a broad-shouldered man in his early fifties with kind brown eyes and a tired expres-sion on his face.

"You're lucky you caught me, Miss Calloway," he said, pushing aside a tall stack of reports so he could see her. "I was about to go off duty."

Star smiled sheepishly. She was already feeling a little guilty about using her own star power to jump to the head of the line. It seemed an awful lot like the kind of thing Eddie Urbane might do. Still, as the saying went, desperate times called for desperate measures.

"I guess I should've called ahead," she said, reaching up and touching her star necklace without realizing she was doing so. "But I was just so excited when Mike told me about the bib that woman found—is it here?" She glanced around the office hopefully, half expecting to see Timmy's bib hang-ing from the coat hook or sitting atop a stack of paperwork. "I'd love to see it. I think I could recognize my mom's stitch-ing—she used to embroider my initials in all my clothes when I went to summer camp."

"Sorry," Kent said. "It's still at the lab. We sent it out for DNA testing, aging, that kind of thing."

"Oh." Star was disappointed. "Um, does that mean you're trying to make sure it's really Timmy's?"

"Yep," Kent replied. "But don't worry—we're expecting to have the results as early as tomorrow morning." He glanced at his watch. "Well, make that later *this* morning."

Star's heart skipped a beat. She was so excited that she could hardly stand it. Once the police got confirmation that the bib belonged to Timmy, the investigation would have a whole new direction to pursue. Her family could be found in a matter of hours!

I was totally right to come here, she thought with a shiver of anticipation. *I'm sure Mike will realize that soon enough. Even if he doesn't . . .* She cut off the thought, not really wanting to finish it. *Anyway, whatever happens, it will all be worth it when I see Mom and Dad and Timmy again.*

Detective Kent stifled a yawn. "No sense either of us hanging around this place all night," he told Star kindly. "Why don't you head back to your hotel and try to get some sleep? We'll call as soon as we know anything."

Star nodded, realizing he was right. The police were busy; she didn't want to get in their way more than she already had. The media already knew she was in Florida, and it was only a matter of time before they tracked her down. The police definitely didn't need a bunch of pushy entertainment reporters making their jobs even harder.

"Okay," she said. "I guess I might as well get some sleep before . . ."

Then she blinked, her voice trailing off as she realized something. Not only didn't she have a hotel lined up, she didn't even have enough money to pay for one. The cash her fans had lent her had barely covered the taxi ride to the station.

Yikes, she thought helplessly. *Guess I'm getting a little too used to having someone else around planning my schedule and paying for everything. I didn't even think about booking a hotel here—I wouldn't even know how to find one! Besides, what kind of hotel is going to let a fourteen-year-old girl check in by herself in the middle of the night? Even a famous one?*

"Um, I'm really sorry to ask," she said to the detective, "but could I possibly use your phone to call my manager? I'll be happy to reverse the charges if you can tell me how to do it."

"Sure thing." Detective Kent picked up the phone. "I'll take care of that for you right now."

Star waited as he dialed Mike's cell phone number. Then

the detective handed her the phone and stepped out of the room to give her privacy as she waited for Mike to answer.

"Mosley here," Mike's familiar voice answered after a couple of rings.

"Hi, Mike," Star said meekly into the phone. "It's me."

She steeled herself for lots of yelling and scolding. But when Mike spoke again, his voice sounded almost eerily calm.

"Hello, Star," he said. "Where are you?"

"I'm in Florida," Star replied. "At the police station. It's like the middle of the night here, and I just realized I don't have anywhere to stay, and . . ." She went on, explaining her predicament.

"All right," Mike said when she had finished. "I'll take care of it. I'll arrange for a hotel and make sure a car comes to pick you up there at the station in a few minutes."

Star swallowed hard. Mike's voice was still calm, but his words sounded oddly clipped and stiff, very unlike his usual easy drawl.

He's really furious at me, she realized, tears springing to her eyes.

"Hey," she said softly, hoping to break through her manager's chilly tone. "Guess what. Detective Kent says they'll have a positive ID on that bib in just a few hours."

"Hmm," Mike replied shortly. "Look, I've got to go. It won't be an easy task to find you a car service in the middle of the night."

There was a click, and the line went dead. Star hung up the phone, blinking back her tears. She was still excited about the possibility of finding her family soon. But even that wasn't enough to keep her mood from plummeting. She'd just realized that she really might have messed things up with Mike for good.

Nine

Star leaned her forehead against the cool glass of the limo window. She stared out at the dark city streets sliding by, trying not to think about the conversation with Mike. It had been a very long day, and she was just too tired to worry about it anymore. Her driver, an older man with smooth olive skin and kind eyes, had greeted her politely upon arriving at the police station but hadn't said a word since.

After about fifteen minutes of winding through the quiet streets, the car slowed down and turned smoothly into a sweeping circular drive, well lit and lined with stately palm trees. A moment later Star saw the glittering facade of a fancy hotel beyond the fronds.

Oh, well, Star thought with a half smile. *At least Mike's not mad enough to check me into the YMCA or something.*

The smile faded quickly as she noticed a large crowd of people milling around just outside the hotel entrance.

Through the limo driver's open window, she could hear shouts as someone spotted the car coming.

"Paparazzi," she murmured with a groan.

Sure enough, as the car glided closer she could see at least a dozen photographers pushing and shoving at each other as they jostled for position on the sidewalk or leaped into the street for a better view. Several flashes went off as photographers snapped pictures of the approaching car.

That's nuts, Star thought wearily. *They don't even know yet if it's me inside or just some business dude on an expense account or something. Besides, who wants to see a photo of the outside of a limo?*

She glanced at her watch. It was just past two o'clock in the morning. She had hoped that the late hour would allow her to avoid the paparazzi crush for once. Just thinking about fighting her way through the crowd into the hotel made her feel more exhausted than ever.

Maybe Tank isn't joking when he calls these guys vampires, Star thought as she looked out at the waiting photographers. *They never seem to sleep, anyway. . . .*

Even though she'd encountered similar situations a million times in the past year, she couldn't help feeling a little nervous this time. It was the first time she would be facing such a big group of reporters all by herself, without a single member of her team at her side—or even Eddie Urbane and his bodyguards. She steeled herself as the car pulled to a stop at the curb.

"Don't worry," the limo driver said, speaking to her at last as he pushed aside the plastic privacy window between the front and back seats. "Your manager told me this might happen. Said he'd arranged for hotel security to meet the car. You just sit tight until they get out here."

"Okay," Star replied softly. Mike had thought of everything—as usual. What would she do without him? She hoped she wouldn't have to find out.

She closed her eyes, glad for the tinted windows of the limo as the paparazzi rushed toward the car. Even though the driver had closed all the windows, Star could hear multiple voices yelling her name.

A few seconds later she heard a different set of shouts. Opening her eyes, she saw that several burly men wearing gold-trimmed dark uniforms had appeared. They waded into the crowd, pushing back the eager reporters, then approached the car. The driver cracked open his window and spoke to them briefly, then glanced back at Star.

"You're good to go," he told her. "These guys will take it from here."

"Thanks," Star said. "Good night."

She took a deep breath as the car door opened. If there was ever a time she wasn't in the mood for dealing with the press, this was it. But she forced a smile onto her face as she climbed out of the limo.

"All right, miss," one of the guards said grimly. "Let's get you inside."

"Thank you," Star said, missing Tank. He took his job seriously, but he also never lost his sense of humor.

She allowed the guard to steer her toward the hotel doors while the others held back the photographers. Though it was tempting to keep her head down and rush straight into the hotel, she forced herself to stop a couple of times to wave and smile for the cameras. She knew that they wanted pictures, and that they would get pictures no matter what. The last thing she wanted was for Mike and the others to turn on PopTV over in Italy and see her looking grim, grumpy, and tired.

Finally she was inside the hotel. The lobby was almost empty. A hotel employee, a plump woman with a slight Spanish accent, was waiting for her.

"Good evening, Miss Calloway," the woman said politely as the guards faded away into the background. "We're so sorry we didn't know in advance that you were coming. I'm afraid we don't have any suites available, so we've had to put you in a single room. I hope that will be all right."

"It's totally fine," Star said gratefully. "All I need is a bed."

The woman nodded. "Thank you for being so understanding," she said. "Your manager asked us to provide a few things for you—pajamas, a toothbrush, and a change of clothes for the morning. Those things are already in the room. But please don't hesitate to call the concierge at any time if you need anything else."

"Thank you," Star said, stifling a yawn. "I'm sure everything will be just fine."

"Wonderful." The woman smiled at her. "Now, if you'll follow me . . ."

Everything, Star thought, almost delirious with exhaustion as she followed the woman toward the elevators. *Mike thinks of everything.*

The next morning Star woke up early to bright sunlight shining in through the window. She sat up and blinked, looking around the small but comfortably furnished hotel room. For a moment she had no idea where she was.

Then it all came flooding back—her escape from the fashion shoot, the flight in Eddie's plane, and her late-night visit with Detective Kent.

She leaped out of bed, almost tripping over a pair of slippers someone had left for her. Slipping them on, she hurried across the room and grabbed the phone on the dresser beside the TV. She called the front desk and was quickly connected with the police station.

Detective Kent wasn't in yet, but the police chief took her call instead. Chief Owensby was a jovial man whom Star had met a couple of times in the early days of the investigation.

"Good morning, Miss Calloway," the chief said. "I heard you were in town. I'm afraid we haven't heard back from the lab yet, but we're expecting the results very soon. We'll call you as soon as we get them, all right?"

Star gripped the phone tightly, flooded with disappointment. Somehow, she had been certain that the results would be in as soon as she woke up.

"All right," she said. "Thank you. I'll be waiting."

She hit the button to hang up, quivering with impatience.

She had waited so long for some real answers about her family's disappearance. How much longer would she have to wait?

It was still early, but Star immediately dialed the phone again. Her grandmother, Nans, always got up early, and Star suddenly ached to hear her comforting, familiar voice. But after nineteen or twenty rings, she had to accept that there was going to be no answer. She tried to call her friend Missy's house next. It wasn't until she heard the *bleep* of the Takamoris' answering machine picking up that she remembered that Missy and her family were at the beach for the week. Star knew she could probably reach her friend there through e-mail or even IM, but somehow that just didn't seem to be enough at the moment.

She flopped into a chair near the window, not sure what to do next. She stared at the phone, willing it to ring. The room was so quiet that she could hear the *chug-chug-chug* of the mini fridge under the desk and the faint *whirrrr* of a vacuum cleaner in some other part of the hotel.

Star jumped to her feet and started pacing. She wasn't used to feeling so alone. Even when she was stuck twiddling her thumbs backstage or facing hours on yet another airplane, she always had someone around to keep her company. She had come to count on Mike's sensible and caring advice, Tank's multilingual quips and funny comments, Mags's impromptu lessons on anything and everything, and Lola's cheerful chatter and companionship. In fact Star couldn't remember the last time she'd been in a position to wish so desperately for the simple sound of a human voice. Even a bark or two from Dudley would have been a comfort at the moment.

She checked the time again, wondering if she should try to call Rome. It would be around lunchtime there; her team was probably sitting around the table in the hotel suite waiting for room service to arrive. Or perhaps they had gone out to some quaint little Italian bistro for lunch. After all, it would be a lot easier for them to go out without having her around drawing attention to their every move.

I wonder what I would be doing if I were there with them right now, she thought, walking over to the window and staring out at the pleasant Florida morning. *What would I have planned for after lunch? Probably sight-seeing or shopping. Or maybe getting ready for one of those TV interviews. . . . I think I was supposed to do a couple of those today. Oh, and we were going to try to meet with that director, Lukas Lukas, and I think some record company people or something like that.*

She winced as she thought about the excuses Mike must be making on her behalf. What was he telling the people who were expecting her? Maybe something like *Sorry, but Star won't be available today after all. She flipped out and went rushing back to the U.S. like a total brat even though I ordered her not to.*

No, Star thought, shaking her head. *Mike's a total professional. He would never say something like that, no matter how mad he might be.*

Wanting to do anything to take her mind off that painful subject, she turned and hurried over to the dresser where the hotel staff had left the change of clothes Mike had ordered. She grabbed them and hurried into the tiny bathroom, turning on the shower as hot as she could stand it.

A few minutes later she was cleaner but no less anxious. As she toweled her hair dry and pulled on the clean clothes, her mind wandered back to Rome. She had really been looking forward to seeing some of the famous sights of the ancient Italian city, which she had been studying in her history and geography lessons with Mags. For a second she wished she could be there right now, wandering around the Coliseum without a care in the world other than what souvenirs to buy for her friends back home.

Then she pictured her parents and baby brother languishing on some deserted island somewhere, with nothing to keep them going but berries and rainwater. They needed her to be here. Didn't they?

Did I make the right decision? she wondered uneasily as she tossed her towel on the sink and headed back out into the main room. *I would do anything to find Mom and Dad and Timmy, of course. But is it really that important for me to be here right now . . . or could Mike maybe have been right?*

For the first time, a sliver of doubt pierced her sense of determination. What if she'd been too impulsive? What if her presence was actually slowing down the detectives' work instead of helping?

She started pacing again, feeling trapped in the small room. She wished she could go out, take a brisk walk through the hot, crowded city streets to clear her head. But it was out of the question; she would be mobbed within seconds if she went out by herself.

Hoping to distract herself, she grabbed the remote control from the bedside table and switched on the TV. She quickly found PopTV, the all-music channel. Star winced when she saw that an Eddie Urbane video was playing, but she left it on. It was better than the silence.

As she set down the remote, she noticed the room service menu. She flipped through it, her stomach grumbling. There had been plenty to eat on Eddie's jet, but Star had been too excited and nervous to feel very hungry. Now, however, she couldn't quite face the thought of making small talk with the room service waiter or signing autographs for the cook's kids. Instead, she wandered over to the mini fridge and peered inside.

Soon she was lying back on the unmade bed, munching on a granola bar as she watched the end of Eddie's video. When the song finished, a pretty, dark-haired VJ named Lucita popped up onscreen.

"Good morning, all," the VJ said in her perky voice. "That was Eddie Urbane's latest. Speaking of Eddie, we have breaking news from the Urbane lane this morning. Seems he's dumped his latest lady, Italian supermodel Capucina, for a hot new crush—he's recently been seen fawning all over fellow teen singing superstar Star Calloway. The new couple just flew back from Europe together, where fourteen-year-old Star is in the middle of her super-successful world tour. Rumors are flying that Star might be joining Eddie onstage when he picks up his own interrupted American tour. Our own ace reporter

Bash is in New York City with the latest on this story."

Star gasped. "*What* story?" she exclaimed aloud. "None of that stuff about me is true!"

Then Eddie himself appeared on the screen. He was standing on a street corner in New York with a few of his bodyguards behind him. The PopTV VJ, a good-looking young man named Bash, was holding up a microphone.

"Star Calloway?" Eddie said with his crooked half-smile. "Of course I know her, dude—haven't you seen the photos of the two of us getting off my private jet in Florida last night? They're all over the papers this morning."

"But yo, Eddie—I'm trying to get the lowdown on the rumors of romance, man," the VJ said. "Is it true that Star is your new squeeze?"

Eddie laughed. "Star and I are just friends. Close friends. She's like three years younger than me, so there's nothing scandalous going on. And even if there were," he added playfully, shaking his finger in Bash's face, "you know a gentleman never kisses and tells." He winked into the camera and smirked.

"You heard it here first," Bash said with a laugh. "Back to you, Lucita."

Star grabbed her forehead with both hands as the picture

cut back to Lucita's smiling face. "What?" she cried at the TV. "I can't believe Eddie said that. It totally sounds like he was hinting that we really are an item, and that's so not true! Why would he say something like that?"

She grimaced as she realized the answer to her own question. Publicity. Mike had told her a million times that Eddie would do anything for publicity.

Her own video, for "Never Give Up," started playing next, but Star hardly noticed. *I guess I should have wondered why he was being so nice to me,* she thought, feeling like the world's biggest idiot. *Ugh! He must be trying to drum up some media coverage for when he starts up his tour again. Or maybe he just wants to make it look like he dumped Capucina instead of the other way around. Either way, he totally sold me out. . . .*

Just then the phone rang, interrupting her gloomy thoughts. She leaped up and grabbed it, immediately forgetting all about Eddie Urbane.

"Hello?" she said eagerly. "This is Star."

"Good morning, Miss Calloway," Detective Kent's voice replied. "How are you this morning?"

"Fine, thanks," Star said, trying to hide her impatience. "Did you hear back from the lab about the bib?"

"We did," the detective said. "I'd rather not discuss it over the phone, though. Would you be able to come back to the station?"

"Of course!" Star exclaimed breathlessly. "I'll be right there."

Less than half an hour later, Star was sitting across a table from both Detective Kent and Chief Owensby.

"First of all," the chief began, "we appreciate how difficult this must be for you—a young girl, missing her family. . . . As you know, we've been working very hard for the past two years to solve this very difficult case, following up on one lead after another. . . ."

Star tapped her toes impatiently under her chair, waiting for the chief to get to the point. She glanced over at Detective Kent, whose face looked rather strained as the chief rambled on for a while about the investigation.

"Yes," Star said, taking advantage of a slight pause when Chief Owensby finally took a breath, "thank you. It's been very difficult. But I'm hoping you have some good news for me now?" She smiled brightly at him, doing her best to hide the anxiety that was threatening to spill over at any moment.

"Ah. Yes." The chief glanced at the other man. "Detective? Why don't you take over from here."

Kent sighed. "No sense in beating around the bush. I'm afraid the test results weren't what we'd hoped," he told Star somberly. "The lab tested the threads used in the embroidery on the bib and found that they couldn't possibly have spent much time exposed to salt water. No more than a day or two at the most, in fact."

Star blinked, not really understanding what he was saying. "But—but what does that mean?"

"It means the bib isn't a real clue. It's just a hoax," Kent said gently. "I'm sorry, Miss Calloway. Someone must have seen those news stories last week, stitched your brother's initials on that bib, and planted it on the beach."

"Don't worry, we're going to track down who did it," the chief put in. "We're already investigating the so-called fan who turned in the bib, and if that doesn't pan out we have a few other leads. Phone tips and such, you know."

"Oh." Star's mind struggled to process this new information. She didn't really care who had carried out the hoax or whether that person was caught. All she could think about was that her family wasn't coming home to her after all. Not anytime soon, anyway.

It was as if an enormous weight were crushing her heart

and her brain, making it hard to think or feel much of anything at all. After a few seconds, though, bitter disappointment came flooding through the numbness.

But I was so sure, she thought. *So certain that we were going to find them this time.* . . . She shook her head, trying to clear the fog and figure out how to feel about what she'd just learned.

Suddenly she thought back to what had happened a week or so ago while she was touring London and Scotland. She'd had a few bad dreams that had made her start to wonder if her family would ever return. For the first time, her optimism had faded, and despair had threatened to take over. But with a little help from her team—including Dudley— she had realized that it was always better to look on the bright side of life.

It's okay, she told herself firmly. *Just because this clue wasn't the real thing, it doesn't mean anyone is giving up. Not the police, and certainly not me. I just have to go back to being patient.*

This wasn't a disaster; it was just a setback. Doing her best to swallow her disappointment, Star smiled weakly at the police officers.

"Thanks for letting me know so quickly," she said. "I really appreciate everything you've done so far, and I know you'll find them sooner or later."

The men exchanged a glance. "No problem," Chief Owensby said. "We only wish we'd known you were coming. We would have made more certain you understood that things weren't definite—regarding the clue, that is— so you wouldn't have had to make the long trip over here for nothing."

"Right," Kent added. "Your manager didn't mention you were thinking of flying in, or I would have told him to hold up at least until the lab got back to us."

Star nodded, feeling slightly foolish. Why had she so completely ignored the advice of the smart, caring adults in her life?

Especially after Mike trusted me enough to tell me about the bib, she thought with a slight grimace. *Guess maybe I'm not quite as mature as he thought.*

Noticing that the policemen were watching her with concern, Star mustered up a smile. "I'm sorry I didn't let you know I was coming," she told them. "It was, um, sort of a last-minute decision."

"I see," Chief Owensby said. "Well, perhaps next time we'll

all try to be a little more clear so as to avoid any more premature moves."

Star felt her cheeks turn pink. Even though the chief's tone was kind and sympathetic, she could tell that he thought that her whole trip had been a waste of time. It made her feel like a dork. Worse, it made her realize that she might have completely alienated her team and lost their trust—for nothing.

"Well, thank you anyway," she told the men politely. "I guess I'd better get going now. I don't want to hold you up any longer."

Kent nodded. "I've been in touch with your manager," he said. "He's already arranged for a flight back to Italy—if you want it, he said."

Star's blush deepened. "Of course I want it," she said quietly. "When do I have to be at the airport?"

"The flight leaves at four," Kent said. "Here, I have the information right here."

Star chewed her lower lip as the detective dug into his pocket. She was already dreading what would happen when she arrived back in Rome. But she knew she might as well get back as soon as possible and face the music.

At least I'll be back in plenty of time for my first concert, she told herself. *It's not for another two whole days.*

The thought made her feel a tiny bit better. Performing on stage was her favorite thing in the world, and it would be nice to have something fun to focus on for a little while. Besides, if she missed the concert and disappointed her fans for no good reason, she knew she would never forgive herself.

Detective Kent finally located the crumpled paper on which he'd jotted her flight information. He handed it over and stood up. "I'll just go call your car," he said. "Excuse me a moment."

He hurried out of the room. Chief Owensby, who was still seated at the table, leaned forward. "I almost forgot," he said with a slightly sheepish smile. "Would you mind signing an autograph for my daughter? She's quite a fan of yours, and I know she'd be just thrilled. Maybe we could take a picture together, too, if it's not too big an imposition?"

"Of course!" Star said, pushing aside her worries. After wasting so much of the police department's time, it was the least she could do. "No problem at all."

"Great!" The chief jumped up, quickly finding her a clean sheet of paper to sign and then tracking down a camera from the station's equipment room. Detective

Kent returned just in time to act as photographer.

"All right," Kent said, peering through the viewfinder as the chief put one arm around Star's shoulders and posed. "Say 'cheese.'"

"Cheese!" Star sang out obediently, doing her best to hide her storm of emotions behind a big, bright, and only slightly fake smile.

Ten

"Thank you," Star told the first-class flight attendant and the pilot politely as she stepped past them onto the ramp leading off the plane. It was a little before eight o'clock in the morning, Rome time, and the freelance security guard Mike had hired to travel with her had spent almost the entire flight snoring in the seat across the aisle. Star hadn't slept much herself; every time she'd started to doze off, her own anxious thoughts had startled her awake again.

As she shifted the strap of her small bag higher on her shoulder, she realized that her hand was shaking. In fact, she couldn't remember the last time she had felt so nervous.

"Ready to go?" the guard asked her with a yawn.

Star nodded. "I'm ready."

But she wasn't sure that she was. *What if Mike didn't even come to the airport to meet me?* she thought as she walked down the ramp with the guard right behind her.

What if he's decided I'm just as self-centered and immature as Eddie and he doesn't want to represent me anymore?

The same sorts of questions had been tumbling through her head nonstop since leaving the Florida police station some fourteen hours earlier.

As Star and the hired guard stepped out of the gate and into the terminal, she glanced around anxiously. Several bystanders noticed her, gasping and calling out excitedly in Italian, but Star had eyes only for her team. Almost immediately, she spotted Mike, Mags, Tank, and Lola hurrying across the waiting area.

Lola saw her and broke into a run. The guard stepped forward threateningly.

"It's okay," Star told him, and the guard nodded and stepped back in time for Lola to brush past him.

"Out of my way, goon," Lola ordered him, flinging her arms around Star. "I need a hug from my girl."

Star laughed out loud and hugged Lola back. "It's okay," she told the confused-looking guard again, her voice slightly muffled by the black-and-white-striped feather boa Lola was wearing over her purple stretch pants and denim jacket. "She's with me."

Tank was the next one to reach her. "Step aside, LaRue," he said with mock sternness. "You're not the only one who missed her, you know."

"Maybe not," Lola responded tartly. "But I'm the one who missed her the most."

But after one more hug, she loosened her grip. As she stepped away, Tank bent over and wrapped Star in his own muscular arms, hugging her so tightly that she was soon gasping for breath.

"Welcome back, Star-baby," he murmured into her ear. "Don't you go scaring us like that again, you hear?"

"O-okay, Tank," she squeaked out between squeezes. She was relieved that Lola and Tank, at least, seemed to have forgiven her without requiring either apology or explanation.

When Tank let her go, she stepped back and glanced at Mags and Mike, who had reached the little group by then. Mike was turned away from her, speaking quietly to the hired security guard. Star bit her lip, wanting him to look her in the eye. That was when she would know where they stood.

But first she looked over at Mags. The tutor was gazing at her with an indecipherable expression on her face.

"Well, Star," she said in the stern tone she normally reserved for hopelessly wrong answers or poor test scores. "The last couple of days have been quite an adventure, haven't they?"

Star hung her head. "I'm sorry, Mrs. Nattle," she said softly. "I didn't mean to worry you. I—I guess I wasn't thinking clearly. I don't blame you if you never trust me again after this."

"All right, all right," Mags said, her voice sounding kinder. "Enough of that sort of talk. You made a mistake, but there's no need to beat yourself up too much about it. There was no real harm done, and I expect you've learned a lesson or two. Yes?"

"Absolutely," Star said, so relieved that she felt tears well up behind her eyes. "Thank you, Mrs. Nattle. It's nice to be back here with you guys."

"It's nice to have you back," Mags said with a smile. "Let's have a hug, all right?"

Star hugged her, burying her face in the scratchy tweed of Mags's jacket. She kept her face hidden there as long as she could, dreading what was coming next.

Finally Mags pulled away, and Star had no choice. She looked up at Mike, hardly daring to meet his eye.

He was looking at her now, gazing down at her solemnly. For once, his face was completely unreadable.

Star held her breath. She was vaguely aware that Tank and the hired security guard were busy keeping curious onlookers away. But she kept her gaze trained on Mike's green eyes.

"I'm sorry, Mike," she said, doing her best to keep her voice steady. "I messed up, big time. I should have listened to you. Can you ever forgive me? Please?" Her voice cracked slightly on the last word.

There was a long moment of silence between them. Star felt like her insides were twisting up into a painful little ball. What if her worst fears were true? What if Mike didn't want anything more to do with her?

Finally Mike sighed and rubbed his mustache. "S'pose this is what I get," he muttered to no one in particular, "working with teenagers." His face broke into a broad smile that made the corners of his eyes crinkle. "It's good to have you home, darlin'," he said, pulling her into a bear hug. "Apology accepted."

Star was so relieved that for a few seconds she just went limp, clinging to him like he was the last life jacket on the *Titanic*.

"Really?" she gasped at last. "Just like that, you forgive me? Are you sure?"

Mike chuckled and pulled back, holding her at arm's

length and gazing down at her. "Of course, sweetheart," he said, sounding surprised. "Was there ever any doubt?"

"Well, maybe a little," Star admitted. "I mean, you told me not to go and I went anyway, and I sneaked out without even telling you, and I know you always said Eddie Urbane was self-centered and I sort of felt like I was being that way too, and . . ." She knew she was babbling, but she was so relieved by the fact that Mike was actually still speaking to her that she wasn't sure she could stop herself.

Mike glanced at the others, then back at Star. "Come here a sec," he told her, pulling her toward an empty bench in a sheltered alcove at one side of the waiting area. "Let's chat." He sat down, and Star perched on the edge of the bench beside him. "Now, what's this all about?"

Star shrugged. "I don't know," she said. "You just sounded so mad on the phone. . . ."

Mike sighed. "Well, I was," he said, staring at her seriously. "But only because I was so dang worried about you. You gave us all quite a fright, disappearin' like that. I thought poor Lola was going to have a conniption when she called me from the photo shoot after you disappeared. She was sure you'd been kidnapped by terrorists or somethin'."

Star bit her lip, shooting a guilty glance in Lola's direction.

"I know," she told Mike. "I feel terrible about putting her through that. And the rest of you guys, too. I don't blame you a bit if you never trust me again."

"Well now, darlin', don't get too carried away there," Mike said. "Sure, I'm not going to forget about this little incident for a while. I'm also going to try not to forget that you're only fourteen, no matter how sensible and mature you act most of the time." He winked at her.

"But you still forgive me, just like that?" Star asked anxiously, still not quite daring to believe it.

"Of course I do!" Mike shook his head, his forehead wrinkling with consternation. "Can't believe you actually thought I might not. How could you doubt it? After all, we're family, right?"

"Right." Star smiled up at him, suddenly feeling buoyant with relief. She reached out for another hug. "Definitely family."

"Dudsters!" Star cried as Tank unlocked the door to their hotel suite to reveal the eager pug waiting on the other side.

The little dog leaped toward her, barking happily. Star bent down and gathered him up in a hug, giggling as he tried desperately to lick every inch of her face with his pink tongue.

"I think the little beast is glad to see you," Tank commented dryly.

"I'm glad to see you, too, Dudley," Star told the pug, doing her best to hold on to his wriggling body. After a few more hugs, she set him down and turned to face Mike. "Okay," she said briskly. "Should we talk about my schedule? How many things do I have to make up? I'm totally willing to give up all my sight-seeing time to make sure I get everything done before we leave Rome." Even though she'd only been away for a day and a half, she knew she had already missed several interviews and other important appointments.

Mags raised one eyebrow at her. "Let's not get carried away."

"Yep," Mike agreed. "You know what they say about all work and no play." He pulled a notebook out of his shirt pocket and flipped it open. "I've already told the studio affiliates we can catch up with them later when we swing through Germany. And Lukas Lukas ended up canceling his trip to Rome anyhow. So all you have to make up is a few interviews and that merchandising meeting. I'm already working on fitting those in."

"Sounds good," Star said.

Mags smiled at her. "Right," she said. "And that should still leave plenty of time for relaxing—and studying. Don't think I've forgotten that we were supposed to finish those word problems yesterday afternoon. Even taking off on an unplanned overseas flight won't get you out of that."

Star giggled. "Oh well, it was worth a try!" she quipped.

"Hey, check it out!" Lola called from across the room. She had switched on the TV, which was set to PopTV, as usual.

Star glanced over and saw her own picture on the screen behind the VJ, along with a photo of Eddie. "Ugh," she said. "Did you guys hear what Eddie's been saying about me? I can't believe it! He—"

"Hush!" Lola hissed. "They're talking about it now."

The whole group drifted over to the TV. Star leaned on the back of the suite's antique sofa as the VJ summarized Eddie's comments from the day before.

". . . but now it seems that either Urbane's hints were untrue, or his rumored romance with Star Calloway was the shortest relationship in the history of the music industry," the VJ said with a slight smirk. "According to our sources, Star is back in Italy, while Urbane has been spotted engaged in a very public display of affection with Xandra Om, the well known new age guru and up-and-coming actress."

The pictures behind the VJ changed. One of the new photos showed Star walking through the Rome airport. The other featured Eddie standing on a busy street corner kissing a beautiful young blond woman in a flowing paisley robe.

Mike snorted. "Leave it to Urbane," he muttered. "He always finds a way to stay in the headlines."

"I can't believe he used our Star to do it," Lola exclaimed, hitting the MUTE button on the TV remote as one of Eddie's videos started playing onscreen.

Star shook her head. "I can't believe I didn't even realize what he was doing," she said. "I thought he just wanted to help me out."

Tank patted her on the shoulder. "Don't be ashamed of that, Star-baby," he said. "You always see the best in people, and that's a fine thing."

"He's totally right," Lola put in. "Don't let a creep like Eddie change your way of looking at the world, babydoll."

Star smiled as Mike and Mags nodded their agreement. "Thanks, guys," she said, with a sudden rush of affection for her whole team. How could she have risked their friendship by sneaking off the way she did?

But I guess it wasn't really much of a risk after all, she realized. *Like Mike said, we're family. That means we can always work things out, no matter what happens.*

She touched her star necklace, thinking of her real family. That reminded her that she needed to e-mail Missy to tell her what had happened upon her return to Rome. She was sure her friend was dying to hear all the details.

"Hey," she said to the adults, who were already wandering away from the TV to different parts of the suite. "If you don't need me for a few minutes, I need to go write to Missy, okay?"

She headed to her bedroom at one end of the suite, Dudley at her heels. Digging into her pocket, Star soon located her handheld, as well as a lollipop she'd picked up in the airport. She flopped onto the bed, unwrapped the lollipop, and popped it in her mouth. Dudley settled down on top of an open suitcase on the floor, making himself comfortable on one of Star's favorite sweaters.

As Star typed in Missy's address, the phone on the bedside table rang, startling her. Without thinking, Star grabbed it.

Because of the lollipop, she couldn't speak for a second. Meanwhile she heard the sharp click of someone picking up another extension elsewhere in the suite.

Mike's familiar voice spoke. "Mosley here."

Star sat up, planning to hang up the phone quietly if the caller turned out to be anyone but Missy or Nans. She listened for the answering voice, more than half her attention already back on her e-mail.

"Good evening, Mr. Mosley," a man's voice said. "Or I suppose it's morning where you are?"

Star's eyes widened. It was Detective Kent!

"That you again, Kent?" Mike's voice responded. "Been meanin' to call and thank you for all your help these past couple of days. I'm happy to report that Star is back with us now, safe and sound."

"Good, good. But that's not why I'm calling."

Star gripped the phone tightly, the lollipop clenched between her teeth. Clearly neither Mike nor Detective Kent realized she was on the line. She knew she should either speak up or hang up. But her entire body seemed to be frozen; she could do neither. Instead she just listened.

"Believe it or not, we've just turned up another possible clue," Kent went on. "Thought you should know about it."

Star's eyes widened. Her heart started beating faster. Glancing down at the snoozing Dudley, she prayed that he wouldn't suddenly start snoring loudly enough to give her away. She felt guilty about eavesdropping, but she couldn't stop.

"Oh, I believe it," Mike said with a wry chuckle. "Now that Star's whole story is public, I'm sure a whole mess of clues are going to start popping up."

Kent laughed. "Yes, well, this one could be a hoax too, of course. But we're checking out all leads carefully."

"So what's the clue this time?" Mike asked.

"It seems some of Star's fans found a message in a bottle on the beach," Kent replied. "They turned it in to us because of the note inside. The words are pretty faded—it looks like it's been out in the ocean for a good long time."

What does it say? What does it say? Star thought desperately.

"What does it say?" Mike asked, as if reading her mind.

"Well, as I said, it's mostly illegible," Kent said. "The only parts we can make out right now are the words *Help, boat, island,* and *baby.* Oh, and the word *Call,* which the fans are convinced is the beginning of Star's last name."

"Are they right?" Mike asked, sounding interested.

The detective sighed into the phone. "Right now, your guess is as good as mine," he said. "Could be, could be not. We're getting some experts in to check out the handwriting and see what they can decipher. We really have no idea if this is connected with Star's case at all. It could be another hoax or a prank—maybe even a publicity ploy by the fans who found it, since they're being interviewed all over the local media already. Or it could just be some random bottle with no connection to anything. It will probably take a while for us to figure it out. But we thought you should know, just in case."

Star's mind was racing at a hundred miles per hour. *Oh, no!* she thought. *If only I'd stayed in Florida a little longer! They don't need experts, they need me! I can recognize Mom or Dad's handwriting if anyone can, no matter how faded it is. Maybe I could hop a flight this afternoon—that way I'd be there by tomorrow morning. . . .*

"I appreciate the call, Detective," Mike said, breaking into Star's thoughts. "Thanks for the update. I don't think I'll tell Star about this just yet—don't want to get her hopes up, after what happened last time. But please keep me posted on further developments."

"I will," Kent replied. "Take care."

There was a click as the line went dead. Star just sat there, still holding the phone receiver.

Hearing Mike's voice had suddenly brought her back to reality. *I can't do it,* she realized, gripping the phone so hard that her fingers started to go numb. *I can't just go rushing off again. I have to sit tight and wait—and trust Mike to tell me when he hears anything definite about this clue or any others.*

She replaced the phone receiver, then stood up and walked over to the dresser. There was a framed photo lying on top: her favorite snapshot of herself with her family. They were all standing on the beach together, smiling and squinting into the sun and looking incredibly happy.

Star's hand moved up to touch her star necklace. How could she possibly ignore what she'd just overheard? She wasn't sure, but she knew she had to try. Mike didn't want her to know about the note yet, and she was determined not to let him down again. She knew that her parents would be proud of her for that. Still, it wasn't going to be easy. . . .

Star stared down at the picture. "Sorry, guys," she whispered to her family. "You know I'd do anything to find you. But Mike is my family now, too, and I have to earn back his trust. And I think this is how I have to do it."